M000113390

Cruising for Murder

A Myrtle Clover Cozy Mystery, Volume 10

Elizabeth Spann Craig

Published by Elizabeth Spann Craig, 2016.

CRUISING FOR MURDER

First edition. August 7, 2016.

Written by Elizabeth Spann Craig.

For my readers. Thank you.

Chapter One

"Okay, I'll watch the house for you while you're away. But I won't watch that witch-cat!"

Myrtle Clover took a steadying breath. She reminded herself exactly why she needed her housekeeper, Puddin's, help. Myrtle was going on an Alaskan cruise with her son, his family and her friend, Miles. This meant someone needed to take care of her house—water the tomatoes, feed her cat, mow her grass. Despite Puddin's complete and utter incompetence, Myrtle must retain her patience and ensure that both Puddin and her husband, Dusty, were onboard.

"Okay then, really all I need you for is to water the tomatoes. But the cat *must* be taken care of. If you want to outsource that to Dusty, that's your own business," said Myrtle.

Puddin raised her eyebrows. "But your house needs cleanin' while you're gone, too."

Myrtle glanced around her living room, allegedly under the tender loving care of Puddin. Dust bunnies had formed rival gangs and threatened to hijack her home while she was gone, turning it into their own personal warren. Every bit of silver she had in the house looked like brass. The wooden furniture was dull from lack of polish. The rug had black cat hair threaded through it.

"If you say so. If you actually *clean* today, it will probably keep just fine until I get back," stressed Myrtle. Because cleaning was never a given when her housekeeper came by.

Puddin, always fond of making herself seem important, said, "I'm going to be very busy, you know. While you're gone. Mr. Miles is having me watch his house, too."

Myrtle narrowed her eyes at Puddin. "Is that so? When I return, I don't want to find out that Mr. Miles's house looks immaculate and mine looks like a victim of the Dust Bowl. You always throw more effort into Mr. Miles's house than mine. It's a peculiar gender bias of yours."

Puddin squinted at her as she usually did when she didn't quite follow Myrtle's line of thought, and changed the subject, another favorite tactic. "Why are you going somewhere cold? You're going to a cold place, right?"

"Alaska? Well, at this time of the year it's probably still pretty chilly, yes," said Myrtle.

"Because the Fourth of July is coming up. And if it was me, I'd be thinking about a cruise somewhere else. I'm thinking the Bahamas. I'm imagining myself in a bathing suit on a beach with a drink with one of them umbrellas in it," said Puddin. "Watching fireworks."

Dumpy, doughy, pale Puddin in a bathing suit didn't bear thinking of. Nor did the fact that Puddin didn't apparently realize that the Bahamas might not celebrate the Fourth of July. Myrtle abruptly asked, "Where is Dusty? I wanted to leave him with some last-minute instructions, too."

Puddin shrugged. "He's around. Probably messing with the mower. Always puttin' oil in the thing."

As if on cue, Dusty, wearing frayed khakis and a grass-stained checkered button-down shirt, pushed open the front door. "Too hot to mow," he muttered to himself as he opened Myrtle's refrigerator and pulled out a pitcher of lemonade. He poured himself a generous glass and, when Puddin, gave a loud, suggestive cough, poured her one too, bringing it to her in the living room where she plopped down on Myrtle's sofa.

"I've had just about enough of both of your foolishness today. Dusty, it looks like an African savannah out there. The grass has to be cut regardless of the temperature. But I'm also concerned about the care and feeding of Pasha," said Myrtle briskly.

Dusty cocked his grizzled head to one side. "Pasha?"

"The black cat," said Myrtle.

"That witch-cat!" said Puddin at a volume guaranteed to make Myrtle's blood pressure rise.

"That will be enough of that nonsense, Puddin. It's an easy enough job, Dusty, and the chore will apparently fall to you since your wife is engaging in histrionics at the thought," said Myrtle.

Dusty grunted at this and eyed Puddin sideways. She had her arms crossed and he clearly knew better than to cross her when she was being obstinate. "All right. What do I do?"

"You let her in at night and give her cat food. You let her out in the morning. You make sure her litter box is in good shape." Myrtle pointed to the stack of cat food cans, the litterbox, and the extra litter.

Dusty grunted again. It seemed to be an assent, although a reluctant one. "That's a lot of coming by," he said.

Myrtle wasn't sure if this was merely a comment or a complaint. "Puddin will be here anyway—taking care of my house and Miles's, too, apparently."

Dusty sighed. He gazed forlornly out Myrtle's front window, gray mustache looking even droopier than usual. "And them gnomes? Can't we move them gnomes at least? So I won't have to be tryin' to mow around them things?"

"I'd rather leave them out there in the yard until I leave. It's important for Red to have a visual reminder before our trip," said Myrtle. When Myrtle pulled her tremendous collection of garden gnomes out, it provided a subtle warning to her son that he needed to watch himself. Considering Red lived directly across the street and considering the fact that he abhorred her gnome collection, it was generally an effective ploy.

Dusty was even a less of a fan of the gnomes than Red. He said, "So when y'all pull out of the driveway I can start luggin' them things to the shed?"

"That's right."

Dusty's relieved smile revealed a dimple that Myrtle had never seen.

The doorbell rang. Myrtle's eyes narrowed with apprehension. "I spotted Erma Sherman lurking out there earlier. I must finish packing and organizing and don't have time for her recitation of all the disgusting illnesses she's inflicted with. Puddin, check the door for me." Myrtle's next door neighbor, Erma, was the bane of Myrtle's existence. Erma's goal in life seemed to be allowing her crabgrass to infiltrate Myrtle's yard, her squirrels to steal Myrtle's birdseed, and to trap Myrtle in conversation.

Puddin, who had settled her pudgy frame into the softness of the sofa, said loftily, "But I'm not your butler."

Dusty started loping toward the door. Puddin, who still suspected Dusty had an odd attraction for the donkey-faced Erma, leapt up from the sofa and waddled to the front door, bypassing her sixty-five year old husband. Peering through the window, she laconically reported, "It's her with some of your mail."

Myrtle sighed and said in a stage whisper, "The mail carrier has been completely demented lately, scattering mail here and yonder. Go ahead and answer the door and report that I'm indisposed."

Puddin squinted at her.

"Say I'm *busy*," amended Myrtle. She fled to the back.

The packing was actually going pretty well. The suitcase was basically ready to go. It was a little tricky packing for a range of temperatures, but since Myrtle didn't have a large wardrobe to start with, it wasn't as much of a chore as it could have been. The carryon was something of a nightmare, though.

"She went away," reported Puddin loudly in a singsong tone.

"Thank heaven for that," said Myrtle fervently.

"Oops, spoke too soon. Knock at the door," said Puddin, continuing the play-by-play.

"And?" asked Myrtle in an impatient voice.

There was a pause where Puddin waddled back out to the living room to peer out. Then, disapprovingly, "It's that woman. Sort of a witch like the cat."

"Oh, Wanda?" Myrtle walked back to the living room. "Let her in."

Puddin disapproved of Wanda, a fact that was written all over her face as she opened the door. Although what Puddin might have to feel superior about was a true puzzle to Myrtle.

"Wanda!" said Myrtle fondly as the skin and bones psychic walked in. Myrtle peered out the front window. "Tell me you didn't walk here again! Wanda, that must stop. It's far too many miles for you to walk here."

"No, Dan gave me a ride. Sort of. Car broke down on the way," said Wanda with a shrug of an emaciated shoulder. "Only had to walk halfway." Crazy Dan was Wanda's brother. They lived at a hubcap-covered hut surrounded by rusted cars that were mostly on concrete blocks. They stuck up homemade signs on the rural highway adjoining their property, promoting their bait, psychic readings, and boiled peanuts.

"Well, let's have Miles drive you back home when you're ready. And Dan, too, of course," said Myrtle. Myrtle's best friend, Miles, had learned with a good degree of horror that he was a cousin of Wanda and Crazy Dan's. "And let's go into the kitchen for a snack," added Myrtle, studying Wanda's thin frame with concern.

Her invitation put Puddin into even more of a snit and she flounced off with her nose in the air. With any luck, she would work off her annoyance with housekeeping.

Wanda carefully pulled out a wooden chair at Myrtle's table and sat with perfect posture as if channeling table manners from childhood. Myrtle peered into her fridge, pantry, and cabinets before finally settling on a variety of different sandwich makings and sides, placing the assorted foods on the table in front of

Wanda. She pulled out two plates, a pitcher of the lemonade that Dusty had unfortunately nearly polished off, and two glasses.

Myrtle watched as Wanda devoured everything set in front of her and provided a monologue in a quiet tone as a background to Wanda's meal. When Myrtle sensed Wanda was filling up, she waited for a minute or two for Wanda to provide the reason for her visit.

"Yer in danger," said Wanda tiredly.

"Naturally," agreed Myrtle in a pleasant tone.

"Shouldn't go on the trip," said Wanda, giving her a sideways look.

"Unfortunately, it's too late to back out now. Red and Elaine are especially excited about the cruise. They've saved up for years to take a vacation like this. Land and sea—Denali and the glaciers. And I'm to help keep an eye on Jack for them from time to time so that they can have a quiet meal or two. Miles and I will play bridge and sip coffees and observe wildlife out the window and it will all be very relaxing," explained Myrtle.

Wanda stared at her.

Myrtle pressed her lips together and then said, "Now, if you're telling me that the ship will end up at the bottom of the Gulf of Alaska, then I won't go and I'll keep everyone else home, too. And I'll call a news conference and tell them a psychic told me the cruise ship would sink and they'll all think I'm demented. Red will incarcerate me in Greener Pastures Retirement Home and breathe a huge sigh of relief. But is that what you're telling me, Wanda?"

Wanda shook her head. "Snow," said Wanda in a fatigued voice, slumping in the kitchen chair a little.

Myrtle nodded in an encouraging fashion as if she understood Wanda's cryptic statement completely. "Snow. Snow, yes."

Puddin flounced in, hands on her hips. "Mr. Miles is here," she announced to the ceiling since her nose was in the air while in Wanda's presence.

Miles walked in. "So you've got a butler now, too?" he asked pleasantly to Myrtle. Spotting Wanda, he automatically put a ready hand near his wallet. Wanda had many needs and, considering the family connection, Miles usually found himself obliging. But Wanda didn't ask, just greeted him in a tired voice. He sat down at the kitchen table with them.

Myrtle said to Miles, "Wanda was just informing me that I was in terrible danger and shouldn't go on the cruise."

"Right," said Miles with the air of someone who has heard this prediction before. "Told you that you should have paid for the trip insurance. You're really just tempting fate, otherwise."

Myrtle kept talking, which was her usual tactic when she didn't like the direction the conversation was going in. "But the ship won't go down; at least Wanda isn't going out on that limb. And she had a tip for me. Snow."

Miles raised his eyebrows. "Plenty of snow on the top of Denali, I'd wager. Not sure how much there might be on the ground."

"True. We're in late June, early July for the trip. Wanda, you can't provide any more clarity than that? Nothing else? Should I at least *seek out* the snow, or *avoid* the snow?"

Wanda shrugged. "The sight...."

"I know, I know," said Myrtle impatiently. "The sight doesn't work that way. Which is incredibly annoying."

Miles opted to change the subject since Myrtle was looking rather tense. "Wanda, what's the plan for delivering your horoscopes while we're gone? I know usually you turn them into Myrtle and she hands them over to Sloan for editing."

Or, more truthfully, Myrtle radically revised Wanda's horoscopes so they more closely resembled English before turning them over to Sloan to be published in the local newspaper.

Wanda shrugged again. "Supposed to bring a heap of 'em to Sloan in a few days." She looked at Myrtle. "Mind if I visit yer restroom?"

"Of course not," said Myrtle in a distracted voice. She was thinking of the horoscopes and Sloan's dismay when he had to figure them out.

As soon as Wanda left, Miles whispered, "You know Sloan won't be able to make heads nor tails of those scribblings of Wanda. She's functionally illiterate."

"She is that," agreed Myrtle. "But she's also completely accurate in her predictions. Odd that they are. And you know that she's the new star at the *Bradley Bugle*. Sloan can't stop publishing her stuff now. And he can't exactly recycle old material—that doesn't work with horoscopes. I'll have to check in with him later. I need to talk to him about my column, anyway."

"Are you all packed?" asked Miles.

"As well as I can be. It sounded as if I might need to dress for different temperatures. I fixed that by packing a couple of sweaters," said Myrtle.

"Did you put in some dressy things for the nice dinners? Aren't we going to have a nice dinner in one of the specialty restaurants one night?" asked Miles. "Although I'm not sure how that will work with a preschooler along. It wouldn't be the kind of restaurant that has crayons and butcher block paper on the tables."

"Oh, there's some sort of kids club or something. Jack will play in there for a little while so that we can skip the buffet line for the main restaurant. He'll be fine in there for one evening. But we have to book it just as soon as we get onboard the ship. Yes, I threw in a dressy top to wear with my black slacks. That will work, won't it? You've been on a cruise before. I'm the one with no idea what to expect," said Myrtle.

Miles said, "I was on a cruise twenty years ago. I wore a white, hand-tied bowtie over a starched white shirt, and a black tailcoat with black dress pants. Nowadays, I'd have passengers trying to give me their drink order."

"Or assuming you were a magician for the kids' club," said Myrtle.

"Anyway, I'm sure you'll be fine, no matter what you're wearing. Someone's hardly going to come up to you and tell you you're dressed inappropriately. You're rather foreboding looking, you know." Continuing quickly before Myrtle could indignantly argue the point, Miles said, "Are you looking forward to it? I know this part is a chore."

"I am. Although there've been moments where I thought *there's no place like home*. Getting the passport ready for flying into and out of Canada, choosing whether or not to do excursions, figuring out the packing. It's been a lot. Then I read up online on the trip. Not official cruise-related websites, but forums."

Miles said solemnly, "Don't ever do that. Forums are full of people with a bone to pick with someone. Seriously, who writes on an online forum unless they're unhappy?"

"These weren't even necessarily *unhappy* people. They were giving their opinion of the trip overall. They just said that the land portion gets a little crazy with all the having to pack and unpack and then label the bags and put them outside your door for the staff to make sure they end up where *you're* going. You have to make sure you cut off the old labels or the staff might send your bags back to a prior location. Can you imagine me replacing all of my wardrobe in a gift shop?" asked Myrtle.

Miles said, "No. No, I can't imagine you wearing an assortment of Alaska tee shirts for a couple of weeks. But Myrtle, we won't be doing that. *You* won't be doing that. You're always perfectly capable of following directions. Our reward will be seeing some interior towns, riding a domed train, and seeing Denali. Denali is supposed to be magnificent."

"I only want to see a bear," said Myrtle plaintively. "That's it. If I see a bear, I can go home happy. I don't ask for much. This won't be a high-adventure trip for me. I'm not going zip-lining or hiking or riding an ATV. But do I want to see a bear."

"From your lips to God's ears," said Miles in the fervent voice of someone who didn't want to hear Myrtle fuss about the criminal lack of bears in Alaska. Then he jumped, eyes wide open.

Myrtle turned to see what had startled him. "For heaven's sake, Miles, it's simply poor Pasha. The dear probably heard herself being maligned by the wicked Puddin." She got up from the table and opened the window a bit to let the cat in. "You stay here with me, sweetie, or else Puddin won't get any cleaning accomplished at all." She glanced at the wall clock. "Where's Wanda? Did she get lost on the way back from the bathroom? Should we check on her?"

Which was exactly the moment Wanda appeared. She reached down to rub Pasha and Pasha rubbed lovingly against the thin woman. "Got to go," muttered Wanda.

"Got to go?" chorused Myrtle. "You just got here! And all you've got for me is *snow*? Usually you've at least got a full sentence for me. *Snow* isn't particularly helpful, Wanda."

Miles said in a more moderate tone than Myrtle, "Can you say if snow is a good thing or a bad thing?"

Wanda thought about it and said, "Good thing."

"All right, excellent," said Myrtle. "Something to work with. And now, do you need Miles to drive you back home? And Dan, if he's sitting on the side of the road?"

Miles looked pained, but willing.

"Guess so," mumbled Wanda, still looking drained. She unexpectedly gave Myrtle and Miles a fierce embrace. "Be careful," she said as she walked out through the front door.

Puddin pushed herself against a wall as Wanda passed, doing her best to keep out of the psychic's way.

"And be careful walking out to Sloan's," added Wanda, sticking her head back in for a second as Puddin once again flattened against the wall, holding her breath so as not to breathe the same air as Wanda.

Chapter Two

I should put the finishing touches on my packing after I take Wanda home," Miles said.

Myrtle was sure that whatever Miles was doing with his packing was basically just shifting things from one side of the suitcase to the other. Miles was so particular and so neat that she knew that the items in his suitcase were color-coded, organized into zipper bags, and were something of a work of art.

Myrtle, on the other hand, felt confident that she at least had everything packed that she needed. Instead of looking at her packed bags one more time before tomorrow, she grabbed her cane for the walk downtown to the *Bradley Bugle* office to see her editor, Sloan.

Her mind wasn't on anything but Sloan. This is why, when she hurriedly yanked open her front door, she gaped at the one person she most didn't want to see there. Erma. Wanda *had* warned her, hadn't she?

Erma Sherman, Myrtle's next door nightmare of a neighbor, grinned at her with that horrid grin. "Where you headed in such a hurry?" asked Erma nosily.

"Business!" said Myrtle. "Got to go. Running late."

"Where? Downtown?" asked Erma. She gave her braying, donkey's laugh. "Must be downtown. You couldn't walk much farther than that, could you? Not being old and whatnot."

Myrtle was quite certain she could walk much farther than downtown, but she wasn't about to debate the point with Erma. Arguing with Erma, she'd learned from past experience, was completely futile in every way.

"You're right about me heading downtown, at any rate. See you later, Erma." And she went thumping off with her cane with great determination.

"Wait! Wait! I'll drive you there. Got to go there myself," said Erma.

Myrtle feared that Erma wanted an audience to listen to her usual recitation of whatever blight she was currently inflicted with. Her illnesses tended to be both repugnant and graphically recounted. Myrtle repressed a shudder. "No thank you. I need the exercise."

"Me too! I need exercise, too!" said Erma in a desperate tone.

This was true. Erma did need exercise. What's more, Myrtle could tell when she'd lost. Wanda had been right—she should have watched out as she left home. Now she was stuck. "All right then. You can walk with me," grated Myrtle behind her clenched teeth.

As she'd guessed, Erma was dying for someone to talk to. Her long-suffering immune system had just successfully battled a bizarre virus with many disturbing side effects, deftly described in some depth by Erma.

Myrtle grimly forged forward. She decided that the best way to combat Erma's assault was by launching one of her own. She settled on a different boorish tactic—talking about one's vacation.

Erma was saying, "The rash, you see, was unbearably itchy and—"

Myrtle broke in, "Did you know that I'm leaving for a cruise?" Of course Erma didn't. Miles and Myrtle would have been the people who told her of it, and they were the ones avoiding her at all costs.

Erma gaped at her. "A cruise? You?" She burst into braying laughter.

"That's right," said Myrtle, bristling now and forgetting her mission to bore the bore. "What of it? What's so funny about that?"

"Only that you never go anywhere! And you don't spend any money. In fact, I don't believe you *have* any money." Erma peered at Myrtle, seeming at last to sense some hostility. "Come on, Myrtle, don't be mad. You know that's true. What kind of cruise is it? Did you win it?"

"I did *not* win it," said Myrtle coldly. "And if I don't spend a lot of money, that's because I like to save it for special occasions. Like this one. I'm going on an Alaskan cruise, as a matter of fact."

"Sayyy," said Erma admiringly. "That should be pretty nice. Are you up for something like that? Isn't there a lot of biking and zip-lining and walking and so forth?"

Not too much farther to the newspaper office. Myrtle said in a stiff voice, "I walk very well, as you can see. I don't, however, think there will be biking and zip-lining in my immediate future."

Erma grabbed Myrtle's non-cane arm, making Myrtle recoil. "Sayyy," she said again. "Is this a romantic trip? Who else is going? Is Miles?"

"Miles *is* going. Since Miles is my *friend*, it does not fall under the definition of a romantic trip. It's a family trip. Red and Elaine and even little Jack are coming along," said Myrtle. She spotted the *Bradley Bugle* office, now looking like a refuge for lost souls, come into sight.

Erma dropped her arm, looking disappointed at losing the opportunity to know some really juicy gossip. "The *baby* is going?"

Myrtle drew herself up and said haughtily, "He's *not* a baby. He's nearly three, in preschool, and completely brilliant. He takes after his Nana—everyone says so. What's more, he's enormously well-behaved."

Naturally, at this moment, Elaine pulled up beside them in her minivan. She rolled down her window, allowing Jack's enraged yells to be released from the confines of the vehicle. Elaine gave a fleeting expression of shock at Myrtle's walking companion, and said quickly, "Need anything from the store, since I'm heading there?"

"No thank you," said Myrtle. "And I'll assume you're torturing my grandson since I was just bragging how well-behaved he is."

Elaine gave a ragged smile. "He is well-behaved eighty percent of the time. The rest is pure toddler angst." She drove away, Jack acting as a siren as they went.

Myrtle was undeterred. "He's ordinarily *very good*."

"If you say so. Okay, well, I'll keep an eye on your house for you while you're gone. Is this one of those 5-day things?" asked Erma, still hoping to hear something negative about the cruise.

"No, it's one of those twelve-day trips with a couple of travel days," said Myrtle, crossing the street to head for the newspaper office.

"Then I'll see you in two weeks!" called Erma as Myrtle quickly walked away.

"Not if I see you first," muttered Myrtle under her breath.

Myrtle pushed open the old, wooden door to the newspaper office. As usual, it took a few moments for her eyes to adjust from the bright sunshine outside to the dimness of the newsroom. It took her even a few more moments before she spotted her editor and former student, Sloan. He was blocked by a teetering pile of old paper, newspapers, and photos. A calendar hanging on a nearby wall was seven years old. It was the land that time forgot.

Sloan scrambled to his feet when he saw her. "Miss Myrtle!" He was a hefty man of Red's age who automatically reverted to guilty schoolboy whenever he saw her. He'd been a completely unremarkable English student when Myrtle taught him. It was still hard for her to wrap her brain around the fact that Sloan was editor of the town's newspaper. Red, in an effort to keep his mother busy, had pushed Sloan into giving Myrtle her own helpful hints column in the paper. Instead, Myrtle wrote investigative pieces as much as she possibly could. Sloan had started out as terrified of Myrtle as if it had only been yesterday that he'd endured her wrath in the classroom. Now, however, he'd grown somewhat more comfortable around her.

"Boy, am I glad to see you, Miss Myrtle. I was worried you were going to fly away for your trip before we had an opportunity for a powwow," said Sloan. He solicitously pulled out a rolling chair for Myrtle, first removing a teetering pile of papers from it.

"The powwow, I'm presuming, is on the subject of Wanda?" asked Myrtle, delicately sitting in the rolling chair, which looked as if it might go careening madly across the room with her in it.

"That's right. It's kind of a delicate situation," said Sloan. His large and ever-expanding forehead starting perspiring.

"Let me guess. Wanda's horoscopes are a hit. However, Wanda's submitted copy is ... challenging," said Myrtle. "Rather indescribable."

Sloan nodded. "Oh, I think I could come up with a few words to describe it. The grammar is so rocky that her sentences sometimes aren't recognizable as English. The only saving grace has been the fact that you've kindly provided your own translation and editing services for the paper."

Myrtle gave a gracious nod.

"And now," said Sloan, tugging anxiously at his shirt collar, "you're heading off for a couple of weeks. I'm not sure that I'll be able to contact you by phone."

"For heaven's sake, *no*! Don't you dare call me. I've got to have some kind of crazy cell phone plan if I receive phone calls or text messages on the ship or on some of those excursions. That would cost me a mint!" said Myrtle, shuddering.

Sloan's face grew even more dismayed. "Then I'm just not sure what I'm gonna do, Miss Myrtle. Could you provide me with some sort of Rosetta stone so that I can make heads or tails of Wanda's physic scribbles? I can't just put her column on a break for a couple of weeks."

Myrtle sighed. "I know. I tried to get her to come up with some horoscopes early so that I could proof them and shoot them over to you. But she told me that wasn't how the sight worked. My only advice to you is to sit down with her when she comes in to deliver them. It's not like she doesn't know she's functionally illiterate. That's no secret. Get her to translate everything and then run it. I'll be back before you know it."

Sloan said, "All right. I guess that's all I *can* do. And speaking of delivering copy, have you got something for me?"

Myrtle pressed her lips together in annoyance. She was ready to move past her helpful hints column and into full-time crime reporting. She loved the long investigative pieces she'd done for the paper on Bradley's various murders. Myrtle was sure if Bradley had *more* crime, she'd have more stories and wouldn't have time to do columns on stain removal.

"I've emailed you something. And I knew that you were going to want a report, a travel article, detailing my cruise," said Myrtle.

Sloan deflated at the word *travel*. "Ah. Maybe you mean a paragraph for our Town Round-Up page? *Marianne Powell is visiting her sister at Lake Hartwell where they plan on getting lots of sun, eating tomato sandwiches, and waterskiing?* That sort of thing?" His face was hopeful.

"Most decidedly *not* that sort of thing. More like a real travelogue, Sloan. Don't worry, it will be *fabulous*. I'm going to take pictures, too, so that we can really illustrate what I'm seeing.People love hearing about great trips and this is a great trip. An Alaskan cruise! There will be bears involved."

"Great," said Sloan. Any enthusiasm faked in his voice was not reflected in his glum features.

The land portion of the trip was indeed fabulous. But it was a whirlwind of towns and modes of travel. They were on buses and vans. They saw Fairbanks, Denali (Myrtle was gratified to see a handful of bears gamboling along the mountainsides), and traveled by domed train to Seward to embark on the ship. She brought a sweater with her for when the bus stopped for photo opportunities, but was surprised to find that it wasn't particularly cold outside. The landscape in Denali was especially remarkable—beautiful, but with a barren quality to it. The trees were stunted because of the permafrost and the unforgiving mountainsides looked lovely but vaguely threatening. Myrtle was glad she was there in the summer since she certainly didn't feel Southerners were good at acclimating to Alaskan winters.

Myrtle was standing next to Miles in the long line to be checked in for the cruise ship. Red, Elaine, and Jack were somewhat ahead of them in line, which was a good thing since little Jack's patience with lines was relatively nonexistent. Miles said with a sigh, "I don't think I've ever been so glad to stay in one place in my life."

"Don't be a fussbudget, Miles. You adored Denali. You'd have liked us to have just left you there," said Myrtle.

"Until winter came, perhaps," said Miles. "And then I don't think I'd like it nearly as well. The scenery has been spectacular, particularly when we could see glaciers from the train. But the part where we had to cut off old labels from our luggage and put on new labels and then stick our bags out in the hotel hall at six in the morning wasn't as much fun."

"You know that frequently we're already up at that point in the day," said Myrtle with her eyebrows raised.

"We may be up, but we're not trying to make major decisions," protested Miles.

"Major decisions like what?" asked Myrtle as they inched slowly forward in the line.

"Like what I'm going to wear the next day and what I'm going to carry with me on the bus or train. Or where my snacks are for the daytrip. Or what simply needs to meet me at my next destination," said Miles, growing anxious just thinking about it.

Myrtle made a *phish* sound and waved her hand. "That's silly. You're remarkably organized all the time."

"Yes, but if I were tired and messed up and didn't cut off the old label, the bags could end up in the town I'd just *left* instead of the place I was heading to."

Myrtle said, "Then you'd just borrow clothes from Red."

This statement appeared to make Miles most unhappy. It was likely because Red did not travel with pressed khakis and immaculate button-downs.

"Now we're here and can relax. We'll gorge ourselves on buffets of wonderful foods. That's what I'm looking forward to now. I've seen the bears. Now I want to see buffets. Because having to buy our own food on the 'land' portion of the trip was pretty pricey," said Myrtle. Then she snapped her fingers. "I know what I meant to do. I meant to put on one of those bracelet things before I boarded."

"Bracelet things?" asked Miles in a bemused voice.

"That's right," muttered Myrtle as she dug through the outside pocket of her carryon. Got to be here somewhere."

"And you were making fun of my zipper bags," said Miles. His eyes were wide as Myrtle pawed through pill bottles for headaches and heartburn, past a charger for some sort of electronic device, before finally locating a terrycloth wristband.

Miles said, "One of *those*, I see. An acupressure wristband to keep you from being seasick. Myrtle, those things are really just placebos, you know. Your seasickness is all in your head and this is a magical-thinking band that keeps you from indulging in the illness."

Myrtle raised her eyebrows at him as she slid it on her wrist. "Be that as it may, I'm putting it on. And I grew up on a lake and boating nearly every day."

After Myrtle and Miles and Myrtle's family had boarded the ship, participated in a very dull lifeboat drill that seemed to upset little Jack in an inordinate and vocal way, and sorted their things in their tiny cabins, they met up for supper, where they feasted their eyes on some of the most delicious food they'd ever seen.

Myrtle sighed. "Smoked salmon. Yum."

They were in a large dining room lined with large windows looking out on the sea. Elaine and Jack finished early and went off to explore the ship—and to give Jack a chance to run any excess energy out.

Red, who seemed a lot more relaxed now that they were all on the ship and finished with their drill, said, "I hear that there's salmon available for every meal. There's a chef who just makes omelets in the mornings and you can even ask that chef to put salmon in your omelet." Red was rapidly putting away a large serving of very cheesy lasagna. Although in his mid-forties, Red was looking younger on vacation than he did as police chief at home. The freckles scattered around his features and his grin reminded Myrtle of when he was a boy. Only the gray in his red hair revealed his age.

"I see weight gain in my future," said Myrtle with a smile. "But then, salmon is good for us. It's going to be tough to return home to my own cooking."

Her eyes narrowed at the swift look transpiring between Red and Miles. Myrtle was aware that there seemed to be some sort of inside joke revolving around her cooking, which was completely ridiculous since she knew herself to be a good cook. She ate her own food *every day*.

Red was always observant, as policemen frequently are. He studied Miles, who was picking at a small salad. "Miles, you've been very quiet. Not that you're usually a loudmouth, by any means. Everything okay?"

Miles took a deep, steadying breath. "I'm fine. Thank you."

Myrtle peered closer at Miles. "You're not fine. You're looking rather green, Miles."

This observation made Miles even greener.

"I've merely lost my sea legs a little," said Miles coldly. "I'll be fine soon, I'm sure."

Myrtle hooted. "You? You said you were an old salt! The water is just like bathwater out there, you know. It's not even choppy at all."

The word *choppy* made Miles appear even more nauseated. "It's only like bathwater if the bath in question contains a hyperactive Great Dane," he muttered.

Red seemed sympathetic. "Well, whatever is behind it, it's miserable. And even old salts can get seasickness. Fortunately, I think Mama came prepared to treat most of the ship for it. Mama, you should run and get him something."

Myrtle gave Red an indignant look. "I'm eating my supper! I'll be happy to help Miles, but the timing isn't perfect right now. I'll be done in a few minutes."

At that moment, a very sharp-eyed old woman with dyed red hair and clutching a cane leaned over their table very close to Myrtle, which startled her. "What's wrong with *him*?" she asked perceptively, pointing a bony finger at Miles. "Seasick?"

Miles looked very unhappy that his condition might be obvious to passersby.

"He's got a touch of it, yes," said Myrtle to the old woman, crossly. "I'll give him something for it, but I was going to finish my supper first." She added in an indignant voice to Red, "You could always go to my room and pick it up. I'll give you the key card."

Red raised his eyebrows. "I'd never dream of rifling through your stuff, Mama. I can't figure out your organizational system for packing. I know there's a method to your madness but if I tried searching for something, I'd mess it all up."

The old woman had dropped her large purse on the table with a clunk and was now methodically searching it. Finally, she pulled out a rather tired-looking acupressure wristband. "Here," she barked at Miles, who was looking increasingly unhappy. "Put this on."

Obediently, Miles slid the wristband over his wrist and gave the woman a tight smile.

"You've got it on wrong!" said the old woman, sounding agitated. "Put the white pressure point over your wrist!"

Miles flushed and finally adjusted the band to the old woman's liking. She gave a sniff and then abruptly said, "I'm Celeste."

Realizing she'd segued into an introduction, Red, Miles, and Myrtle introduced themselves.

Miles asked politely, "Are you traveling with anyone?"

"I'm here with my worthless family," said Celeste darkly. "Husband, son, and daughter. And I've also got my niece, who takes care of me, and a friend."

"Large group," said Red. "Is there a special occasion?"

"No special occasion. My family are leeches. Absolute leeches. I planned a trip to Alaska and they *had* to come along. Worthless," said the old woman, eyes burning.

Myrtle noticed the old woman didn't appear to have the money to foot the bill for that many people to go on an Alaskan cruise. She wore polyester pants that swung on her bony frame. She wore a long sleeved shirt that hung on her. Her dyed hair was unkempt and looked as though it'd never met a comb. She had sensible shoes on that seemed to be at least a decade old—that's because Myrtle was fairly certain she had owned a pair just like them. But appearances could be deceiving.

"Do you play bridge?" asked Celeste sharply, swinging her head around so that she was right in Myrtle's face.

Myrtle swallowed the last bit of smoked salmon. "Of course. Isn't it mandatory that everyone our age plays bridge?"

The old woman peered at her through narrowed eyes for a moment before giving a hooting laugh. "That's funny. You'll be all right to hang out with. And you can meet my friend, Bettina. She's a card. We'll have a good time," said the woman in a peremptory voice. She abruptly left, saying over her shoulder, "Meet us in the parlor area of the ship, near the piano bar tomorrow afternoon."

"That's rather annoying," said Myrtle, staring after her. "She didn't even give a time. Afternoon spans quite a while, you know. And I'm not at all sure that *she* will be 'all right to hang out with'. She's entirely too bossy."

Red said, "Well, Mama, there's really not a lot else to do tomorrow. We're at sea so there are no excursions or anything. Besides, she might be a good one to keep an eye on."

Miles, who was already looking peppier, said, "In what way? You think that the family situation she was talking about sounded like trouble?"

Red said, "I sure did. Although Celeste didn't seem like the kind of person to allow herself to be pushed around."

"True," mused Myrtle. "All the same, it's an interesting set-up. I might keep my ears open to hear more about Celeste's crazy family." She glanced over at Miles and said wryly, "You could come with me, Miles. I know how much you enjoy playing bridge. And you certainly seem a lot better, despite the fact that you were saying my band had a placebo effect."

He had the grace to blush.

Chapter Three

Everyone turned in early that night after the long day of travel. Although Myrtle was usually plagued by terrible insomnia, she slept soundly with the ship rocking her to sleep like a baby. She did wake very early in the morning, though, and checked her watch, making a face. It was too early to even get a buffet breakfast. She decided to get ready for her day, dress, and explore the ship for a while before eating.

When she opened her cabin door, she smiled. It was a pleasure to walk out a door and not have to see if Erma were outside, stalking her. Even better, Miles was carefully closing the door to his stateroom so that it wouldn't make much noise for everyone still sleeping on their hall.

"Did you sleep?" asked Myrtle in a quiet voice. "And are you feeling well?"

"Surprisingly, I slept. And even more surprisingly, that woman's wristband seems to be doing some good. I was hoping for breakfast," said Miles as they walked down the long hall, made a sharp turn, and walked down another long hall.

"You'll have to keep on hoping because they don't open the buffet until seven. But the upside is that we'll probably be the only people there and don't have to wait in any lines. I want to go to that omelet maker and have an omelet with salmon in it," said Myrtle, a gleam in her eye.

"You're becoming fixated on salmon," murmured Miles. "Must be because of all the salmon-eating bears you saw."

"It's not like daily salmon is an option in Bradley. That's one reason I wanted to see bears. You don't see bears every day in

Bradley, either. And thank heavens for that or else I'd have to put poor Pasha up in the house," said Myrtle.

"Hardly an option for a feral cat," said Miles. "What's our plan? We're not going to hover hungrily in the dining room watching them get the food ready, are we?"

"Certainly not. We'll tour our ship. I want to see all the different promenades. And maybe look out the window, too. It's broad daylight practically all the time here. Maybe we can see whales," said Myrtle.

The ship was tremendous and it took a while for them to see the dining rooms, the bars, the disco, the gym, the pool and hot tubs, casino, auditorium, and the basketball and tennis court.

"I might want a nap after this," said Miles.

"It's just fascinating to me," said Myrtle. "It's like a city on the sea."

"A city of sleeping people," said Miles. "I have a feeling a lot of these passengers stay up very late at night."

"There did seem to be a lot of hubbub out there last night," said Myrtle. "But I couldn't say that I was interested in anything but sleeping."

Miles nodded his head over to the left. "If you had, maybe you'd have ended up like that guy."

Myrtle looked over and made a face. There was an attractive older man around Miles's age in the piano bar. He was sound asleep in a very uncomfortable-looking position in a tall-backed armchair. His mouth was open in a snore and beside him on the floor was an empty glass with a red cocktail straw in it.

"Most definitely *not* like that," said Myrtle. "I have a feeling he has overindulged."

As they watched, a thin, mousy-looking woman of around thirty wearing glasses too large for her face, came hurrying up to the older man. "Randolph!" she said urgently, pulling at the man's jacket sleeve. "You need to go back to the stateroom. Celeste is mad!"

Myrtle and Miles looked at each other with raised eyebrows. Surely that must be the same Celeste they'd met the day before.

The man blearily opened an eye, stared at the woman, and then allowed his eye to sag closed again. The younger woman yanked at his arm this time, pulling him up out of the armchair. But his weight was too much for her to bear and he dropped back down.

Miles, ever gallant, strode over. "Allow me to help you," he said politely. He heaved the man up by the arm and slung the arm across his shoulders. The woman stood on the man's other side and supported him there.

"Thank you so much," the woman said gratefully. "I don't think I could have gotten him back to my aunt's stateroom. And she's dreadfully mad at him. The longer he's away the angrier she'll be."

Myrtle, always interested in a story, said, "I'll follow along for moral support. I think we may have met your aunt yesterday. Celeste is an older woman, like me? And you're traveling in a fairly large group? I'm Myrtle, by the way, and this is my friend, Miles."

"I'm Eugenia," said the woman. "And yes, that sounds like Celeste. I'm her niece and this is Randolph, her husband."

Randolph groaned a bit at the sound of his name. Or perhaps he was groaning at the mention of Celeste.

"But you've got more in your party, don't you?" asked Miles. He was slightly breathless and sounded to Myrtle as if he were valiantly trying to conceal that fact.

"That's right. We've also got her son Terrell and daughter Maisy with us," said Eugenia.

Myrtle added, "And her friend, isn't that right? I can't remember the friend's name, but we were to play bridge this afternoon."

"Yes—Bettina. And that's most certainly Celeste you met if you were planning on playing bridge. But be careful. She's quite the card shark," said Eugenia with a slight smile on her face.

Myrtle said, "Celeste walked away without telling me what *time* I'm to be playing bridge with them."

"That sounds likely. She usually plays around three o'clock, so I'm guessing she'll try to keep to her schedule while she's traveling." Eugenia paused as Randolph sagged a bit and hefted him back up again.

Miles was now definitely winded. He wheezed to Randolph, "Look here. See if you can help us a little." There was no response from the man. Miles stopped and shook his burden a bit. "Look here!"

This prompted a slight reaction from Randolph. He opened his eyes, at least.

"Stand *up*," ordered Miles.

Randolph stood, weaving slightly in place. Miles and Eugenia each took an arm and they continued slowly down the hallway. Apparently, Celeste and Randolph were on the same deck as Myrtle and Miles, and along the same hallway.

Myrtle said, "So, Eugenia, are you just the best niece ever? I thought you said that Celeste had a daughter and a son along on this trip. Why aren't they helping?"

Eugenia flushed. "No, I'm not the best niece ever, I'm sure. But I live with my aunt and help her out. Sort of a companion, I guess. Like they had in the old days. Oh, here's the room. Thanks so much for your help." She fished Randolph's key card from his jacket pocket and managed to propel the man inside the stateroom. Celeste's angry voice could be heard just seconds later.

Miles said, "Let's hit the breakfast buffet before it gets busy. It opened a few minutes ago."

Myrtle nodded, walking thoughtfully. "You know, I don't think Miss Eugenia is a companion at all. I bet she's more like a servant."

"That's a leap, isn't it? We haven't even seen the two of them together," said Miles. He hit the button for the elevator.

"True. But really ... what kind of married woman has a companion? Shouldn't her *husband* be Celeste's companion?"

Miles said dryly, "If he's drunk or hungover all the time, maybe he isn't fit for companionship. Oh, look at the mat." He pointed to the floor of the elevator where the staff had thoughtfully laid a mat with the day of the week emblazoned on it.

"Nice reminder," admitted Myrtle. "This is a place where it's easy to lose track of time."

That afternoon, after having eaten both a tremendous breakfast and a tremendous lunch, Myrtle knocked on the door of Miles's cabin. "I need to do something very, very ordinary," she said in a serious voice.

Miles opened the door to let her in. "I was just watching *Tomorrow's Promise* and feeling a little guilty about watching TV on a cruise ship."

Myrtle settled onto the small sofa in the cabin. "Why should you feel guilty? We've had plenty of fun today. We toured the ship and I took lots of pictures for the *Bradley Bugle* exclusive. We looked obediently out the windows or portholes or whatever when someone on the intercom spotted wildlife outside. We've eaten *salmon*. At every meal today so far!"

"And dessert at each meal," said Miles thoughtfully. "Even a sugary snack. And a glass of wine upstairs after lunch."

"We have *lived* today! So if we want to decompress from the overwhelming amount of fun we've been having to watch a soap opera, we should do that. That's what vacation is all about," said Myrtle, thumping the sofa beside her to emphasize the point.

But they did both jump as if they were doing something to feel guilty over when there was a knock at the door.

It was Elaine with toddler Jack in tow. She beamed at them. "What a good idea to watch some TV! I think I'm going to have to turn on the set in a little while just to give Jack a chance to wind down some."

Jack ran over and Myrtle gave him a tight hug and a kiss on the cheek. "I saw you walk through when Miles and I were having a glass of wine after lunch."

"Walk?" asked Elaine wryly. "Or jog?"

"There might have been some fast walking involved," said Myrtle with a smile. "What have you two been doing so far?"

"Red and I are going to switch off in a little while and I'm to get a massage in the spa," said Elaine. The look on her face said that she was greatly anticipating this appointment. "While we're at sea and there are no excursions, I'm just trying to take advantage of what's available on the ship."

"A good tactic," mused Miles. "I could use one, myself. Maybe while Myrtle is playing bridge this afternoon."

"You've got a bridge partner? Already?" asked Elaine with a grin. "That's fast work."

"Oh, well. She seems to be a horrid harpy card shark, but I'm going to give it a go. Thought I'd try to have a quieter, less-extraordinary day today," said Myrtle. "And remember I can watch Jack for you and Red tonight so that you can have a nice dinner together. I'm just as happy to fill a plate at the buffet early and eat in the room. Jack and I can be couch potatoes together and watch some TV."

"That would be *perfect*. A perfect end to a great afternoon," said Elaine.

After Elaine and Jack left, Myrtle and Miles watched the rest of their show and then Myrtle headed off for bridge. Celeste was sitting with an attractive, tanned older woman who wore a lot of gold jewelry, while niece Eugenia hovered nearby. Myrtle supposed that the woman with the jewelry was the friend Celeste was traveling with.

As Myrtle approached, she saw that the man sitting at the table was the one that they'd helped to his stateroom that morning—Randolph. He glanced at her with absolutely no sign of recognition whatsoever. Considering his condition that morning, this was probably to be expected. He didn't look as though he felt all that well now.

Celeste barked at Myrtle, "There you are. Glad you finally made it. Needed one other person."

Myrtle raised her eyebrows and glanced pointedly at the group. "Did you? It looks like you've got a full foursome to me."

Celeste waved a bony hand in a dismissive way. "Not this group. Eugenia is pathetic at bridge. Randolph is so hungover that he's useless. My daughter is going to join us in a minute—she's got half a brain even though she's morally bankrupt."

Randolph snorted and then took a long sip from his glass. Myrtle observed that it appeared to be a cocktail. He saw the direction of her gaze and said laconically to her, "Hair of the dog."

"It's only hair of the dog when it's morning, you idiot!" snapped Celeste.

Randolph said, "Feels like morning." He stood up, staggering away with a muttered, "Restroom."

"You can see what I have to deal with," said Celeste. Like yesterday, her frame was lost in a pair of baggy polyester pants and top. She wore a shawl and a sour expression.

"It seems like a lot," agreed Myrtle. Randolph, at any rate, was completely unimpressive.

"Eugenia!" said Celeste, making the woman jump at the sharp tone.

"Yes? Sorry?" she asked.

"Can you chase down Maisy for me? Where *is* that girl? She was supposed to be here ten minutes ago," said Celeste.

Eugenia scurried away with Celeste barking after her, "Hurry! Faster!"

The woman with the gold jewelry gave Myrtle a broad smile that didn't quite meet her eyes. She held out a tanned hand to

Myrtle for a surprisingly firm handshake. "I'm Bettina," she said. "A friend of Celeste's."

"How nice for you both to be able to travel together," said Myrtle.

"It's a lifesaver, that's what it is," muttered the unhappy Celeste. "Imagine if I'd had to be stuck with my family."

Bettina grinned at Celeste, but Myrtle noticed again that it didn't seem sincere. "At least you'd still have help. It's good to have help."

Celeste gave a hooting laugh. "Some help. Maisy is always running off somewhere and she's been dressed completely inappropriately since we got on the ship. Randolph is usually smashed and tumbling out of chairs. Terrell is equally useless— besides, he wants nothing to do with me."

"That's her son," explained Bettina to Myrtle. "True, but you'd still have Eugenia, who's worth more than all of them."

"Eugenia," said Celeste, "is poor as a church mouse. She's hardly helping me out of the goodness of her heart but because she's functioning as an employee. Plus, she's slow."

"She seemed to be scampering off pretty quickly to me," said Myrtle.

"No, I mean she's slow *mentally*. Not much of a companion," said Celeste.

Bettina snorted. "She's not *slow*, Celeste. For heaven's sake. She's just not quite as sharp as you are. *Nobody* is quite as sharp as you are." She turned to Myrtle and regarded her through heavily mascaraed lashes. "I hope you have your wits about you. Celeste is a card shark."

"Lies," muttered Celeste. She squinted off across the ship, looking for Eugenia and the errant Maisy.

Bettina leaned closer to Myrtle and said confidingly, "The thing is, Celeste is so clever that she gets bored. She likes to play games. That sort of thing."

"I'm going to look for them, myself," said Celeste darkly. "Be right back."

As Celeste stomped off, Myrtle said to Bettina, "What kind of games are you talking about? I'm assuming you're not talking about Monopoly and poker."

"Oh, I've no doubt she'll be in the casino, but mainly just to drag Randolph out of there. When he gets sloppy drunk, sometimes he feels lucky with the cards. Pity that he rarely is," said Bettina.

Myrtle said, "Celeste paid for this vacation for her whole family ... is that right?"

Bettina grinned at her, revealing a gleaming set of teeth. "I'm guessing you're referring to the fact that Celeste dresses like a peasant. It's true. She's always gone for a very understated look and I don't think she's ever really cared about her appearance. But yes, she's loaded. Believe me."

They turned at the sound of a loud argument taking place behind them. But was it really an argument if only one person was shouting? The person shouting was a plump, middle-aged woman with very blonde hair and too much makeup. Celeste was simply listening, leaning in on her cane with a cold hostility.

"I'm *not* playing bridge, Mother. I told you. I'm hanging out with Guy."

"Who is *Guy*?" asked Celeste, condescension dripping from her words.

"He's the person I've been seeing since we boarded the ship," said Maisy at increased volume as if her mother were hard of hearing. Which Celeste didn't appear to be at all.

Celeste was staring at Maisy as if she didn't even recognize her.

Bettina said in a gossipy voice under her breath, "Maisy doesn't ever behave like this. This is very, very defiant of her. She depends on Celeste for *everything*. And Celeste usually has her under her thumb."

Maisy certainly didn't appear to be under Celeste's thumb now. In fact, she was walking away from her mother as fast as she could. Maisy said loudly over her shoulder in a snarky tone, "Ask *Terrell* to play bridge! Or don't you want to disturb the delicate genius?"

Bettina winced. "Maisy is being ugly about her brother, but they usually get along. He's a physician."

Celeste came walking toward them quickly, cheeks red with anger. Bettina quickly assumed a casual position as if she and Myrtle had overheard nothing.

Celeste sat down with a thump. Eugenia, who'd been hovering nervously in the background as Maisy yelled at Celeste, clasped her hands together and looked even more anxious.

"Here," said Myrtle, "it's hardly the end of the world. We need one additional player. We can either use Eugenia," (Celeste made a face), "or I can run and get my friend, Miles, to participate. He's a very decent bridge player, although I thought he was going to have a massage during this time."

Celeste said, "I choose Miles."

Fortunately, Miles had found that the spa was completely booked up, as was apparently common during the 'at sea' days. He made a good fourth for the group and the anxious Eugenia was sent back to her stateroom.

Celeste said, "That was just an example of some of what I have to deal with. Maisy is completely worthless. Eugenia is nearly as worthless, although it's not for want of trying. My son is ungrateful. Randolph, my husband, is a total disaster."

Bettina grinned at Celeste after her litany of problems. "But you've got me."

"True," said Celeste with a small smile. But she had a cagey look in her eyes as she quickly changed the subject. "So, Myrtle, what do you do? You're old, so I'm assuming the answer is 'play bridge and watch TV?'"

"Certainly not! At least, not all the time," said Myrtle, annoyed. "I'm an amateur detective. I've solved quite a few murders in my hometown."

Celeste looked at her sharply. "Is that so?"

Miles cleared his throat. "I'll corroborate that. Myrtle seems to have a rare gift for crime fighting."

Celeste continued to consider this while Bettina was ready to talk about other things. She said, "So, are you two excited about tonight? I'm dying to talk about it and I know Celeste doesn't care one whit."

Myrtle and Miles looked blankly at each other and then at Bettina. "What are you talking about?" asked Myrtle.

"Don't you know? They're filming a movie here, that's what! Most of the scenes will be shot away from the other passengers, of course. I guess they'll be blocking off some areas while they film at specific locations. But tonight they're filming in the big auditorium and they need passengers to be there for extras," said Bettina.

Myrtle shrugged a shoulder. "I'm not so interested in films. I never even see them until they make it to TV."

Miles said, "And by that time, the fact that there are commercials stuck into the most exciting parts takes all the tension out of the movie."

Bettina didn't look at all deflated. "Maybe, but how often do you get the chance to be *in* a film?"

Miles asked politely, "Who are some of the actors in it? Maybe Myrtle and I know them."

When Bettina listed the names, however, Myrtle and Miles exchanged baffled glances. Apparently, they were more out of pop culture than they'd realized.

"And there's also Samuel Kingston," said Bettina, as an afterthought.

Little did she know that she'd finally struck gold.

"Sam Kingston?" asked Myrtle, sounding a lot more interested.

"The one who's on *Tomorrow's Promise*?" asked Miles.

Bettina raised her eyebrows. "Have I finally struck a chord?"

Myrtle said, "Miles and I watch the show."

Miles blushed, as he always did when his soap opera viewing habits came up.

Myrtle continued, "But what time are they filming? I'm babysitting around suppertime."

Bettina said, "Oh, you know how filming is." Her voice implied that she knew all about it. "They have to have a million takes of a scene. It'll likely go on forever and I bet you can slip in at any time. But it starts at seven."

"That's fine then. Red and Elaine will be back from supper. Miles and I will look out for you, Bettina. And Celeste? Are you going?" asked Myrtle.

"Nope. Can't stand that kind of thing. Going to eat myself into a coma at supper and then go to bed," said Celeste. She gave Miles a searching look through narrowed eyes. "Did you stop being nauseated? Still wearing my band."

Miles winced at the reference. "I am, actually. It does seem to help. Did you need it back?"

"Nope! I'm fit as a fiddle. And now, can we get on with it? I want to focus on the cards," said Celeste.

Celeste, naturally, won. And Myrtle and Miles were both eager to escape her negative presence by the time the game ended. But before Myrtle could get away, Celeste had grabbed her arm with surprising strength and pulled her to one side.

"I need to tell somebody this," she said in her rather scratchy voice. "And if you're really a detective, you're the one to tell."

Myrtle shifted a little uncomfortably. "The keyword there was *amateur*. *Amateur* detective. Sleuth, really."

This didn't seem to sway Celeste. "Whatever. So listen. My life is in danger. I'm sure of it."

"By whom?" asked Myrtle.

"If I knew, I'd get them arrested. I have no idea. One of my worthless family members, at any rate. I've spent so much time with them recently on this trip that I've drafted a change to my will," said Celeste.

"Is that legal? I mean, does it count? Some scribblings on a paper? I thought we had to make a major financial investment through a lawyer," said Myrtle. "And have witnesses."

"It's a holographic will. Look it up," snapped Celeste. "The cabin stewards witnessed for me."

Myrtle frowned. "I thought that was some sort of 3D image."

Miles had interrupted their little tête-à-tête. "No, that's a holo*gram*. Close, though."

"Anyway! Getting back to the point," said Celeste. "I've rewritten my will. Because some people would rather me *not* rewrite it, I've hidden it. It's pinned inside one of my dresses. In case something happens to me, I thought someone should know."

And with that, she walked away with no goodbye.

Chapter Four

Elaine was beautifully dressed in an off-the-shoulder black gown and Red looked rather dashing in a dark suit when they knocked at Myrtle's door to drop off Jack. Jack ran in and hugged Myrtle around the leg.

Elaine said apologetically, "He's been sort of fussy this afternoon and didn't want to take a nap. If you have any problems, just call the restaurant."

"Problems? With Jack?" Myrtle made a scoffing sound. "He and I always have fun, don't we Jack? We're going to play a little and then we'll watch a little television. I'm going to show him how to make a snowflake out of folded paper and scissors."

Red looked extremely dubious about this. "Scissors and toddlers aren't the best combination, Mama. He's likely to cut his hair. Or yours."

Myrtle put her hands on her hips. "He certainly won't! What nonsense, Red. These are safety scissors and they'll barely cut through paper. You'd think I'd never raised children! Now off with you."

"You've had something to eat?" asked Elaine, still hovering.

At that moment, a voice behind them said, "Room service."

Myrtle smiled. "I believe Miles has decided to join me for supper in my room."

Red shook his head and stepped out of the way so that Miles, carrying a tray laden with different types of foods, could pass by. "Miles, I hope you know what you're in for. This is a tiny little room for two adults and a toddler. Believe me, I know."

"It'll be fine. We'll eat so much that we'll all be sleepy," said Miles.

"Thank you both!" said Elaine fervently and she and Red left for their dinner.

"There better not be any sugar on that tray," said Myrtle, peering at the tray. "If we're to get sleepy after eating, that is."

"Naturally," said Miles. "I only brought some crackers for Jack. Sugary treats and tiny staterooms don't match."

As Myrtle suspected, everything went perfectly well. Jack ate, they made snowflakes, and then they watched television. Miles dozed off and Myrtle finished the crossword puzzle that was on the back of the ship itinerary that had been delivered that morning. Jack was always an angel when Myrtle watched him. She didn't believe Red and Elaine's tall tales of Jack's exploits.

Red and Elaine collected Jack in what seemed like record time and it was just Myrtle and Miles again.

"So—the filming, right?" asked Miles. "That sounded like the best bet for us from tonight's entertainment options."

"Yes, it definitely beat the dance competition and the piano singer," said Myrtle. "But I've got to change if we're all supposed to look as if we just came from dinner. That's what Bettina had said, anyway."

"I'll change, too," said Miles, although he looked perfectly fine in his button-down shirt and dark pants. "I'll be back in a few minutes."

Myrtle put on a pair of dressy black slacks and a turquoise top. When she was smoothing down the top over the slacks, she heard a crinkling sound coming from one of her pockets. She reached her hand in with a frown. The slacks had been laundered before the trip so why was there paper in the pocket now?

She pulled out a torn-off bit of legal paper with a highly recognizable but nearly illegible scrawl on it. "Wanda!" she muttered to herself. Myrtle found her reading glasses and plopped down on the small sofa to peer at the paper under the light.

The paper said: *sumtimz drinkin iz dedli*.

"What on earth?" murmured Myrtle. She remembered that Wanda had spent a good deal of time in Myrtle's bedroom area where her packing was taking place.

There was a light tap on her door and Myrtle opened it to Miles.

"Ready to go?" he asked.

Myrtle grunted. "In a second. Here, look at this." She passed him her reading glasses and the note.

Miles, looking rather unusual with flowered reading glasses on, studied the paper. "Wanda's handiwork, I presume. Where did you find it? Is she employing carrier pigeons to deliver now?"

"It was in my pant pocket," said Myrtle with some consternation. "I'm guessing that she stuck a message in there when she left us to use the restroom."

"What do you think it means?" asked Miles. "Do you suppose that she's talking about the drunken Randolph? He's the only person I've seen so far that consistently overindulges."

"I guess. But why tell us about it? It's not like something we don't know, either—drinking *is* bad for you," said Myrtle.

"Yes, but she doesn't stop with the 'bad for you.' Wanda says it's deadly. So do you think we are supposed to warn Randolph to take it easy with the liquor? Or warn someone around him?" asked Miles.

"And what exactly are we supposed to say? That a functionally illiterate psychic from the American South stuffed a ratty piece of paper in my pocket before we left? That her prophecy indicates Randolph might die from drink? They'd think we were nuts. Besides, it doesn't specifically mention Randolph. No, I think we just keep our eyes open and think about it," said Myrtle. "And now I'm ready to gape at one of our favorite *Tomorrow's Promise* actors."

There were many, many people who'd apparently decided that the filming constituted the very best on offer for the shipboard entertainment that night. It *was* interesting to get a behind-the-scenes glimpse of the process. And it *was* interesting to see this actor get direction or take breaks or generally just act like a real person. But it was tedious. There were many different takes.

During one of the breaks, Myrtle said, "I think I'm going to take a restroom break and not come back. I've seen everything I need to see. And I don't think we're going to be able to run into Bettina or anyone else in this madness. There are so many people attending that there's no way to find anyone."

"There must be about seven hundred people here," agreed Miles. "Not half the passengers, but close to it. I'm with you—let's call it a night. Tomorrow is Glacier Bay and I want to be up early enough to reserve a spot at the window in the upper-level lounge."

Miles and Myrtle were walking down the narrow hallway to their rooms when a wild-looking Eugenia leaped into the hall. She spotted Miles and Myrtle approaching and hurried up to them. "She's gone," Eugenia gasped.

"Who? Celeste?" asked Myrtle with a frown.

"Yes. I went in to check on her and she's not in her cabin. I like to make sure my aunt is settled at night before she goes to sleep," said Eugenia. She was clasping and unclasping her hands as if to keep them from fluttering away.

Miles said, "Maybe she was hungry and left for a snack. They have snacks set up near the pool deck. I could walk there with you."

But Eugenia was shaking her head, setting her glasses askew. Her voice was anxious as she said, "But she wouldn't do that. My aunt always follows the same evening routine. She turns in at exactly the same time. She doesn't like changing anything around. And she says eating after supper gives her indigestion and prevents her from sleeping."

Eugenia seemed well-versed on what Celeste said. "So you're saying it's extremely out of character. And you've been in her cabin. Do you mind if Miles and I take a look?"

Eugenia shook her head. She put the room card into the door with shaking hands.

They walked inside. Myrtle exclaimed, "But it's a mess in here! Was there a scuffle?"

There were papers scattered on the bed and desk. Celeste's suitcase had been pulled out from under the bed and put in the middle of the floor.

Miles asked, "Is Celeste usually untidy?"

"No. But sometimes Randolph makes a mess," said Eugenia with a shrug. "But when he does, Celeste asks me to come right in and clean it up. She doesn't like living in any type of disorder."

"Is anything *missing*?" asked Myrtle.

"My aunt," said Eugenia dully.

Myrtle recalled that Celeste had said Eugenia wasn't the brightest bulb in the package. "Besides your aunt. Is anything *else* missing?"

Eugenia looked around the messy room with a dazed expression on her face. "A champagne bottle. There was a large bottle of champagne on the desk."

Miles said, "Randolph likely took it."

Eugenia shook her head adamantly again. "No. No, he'd *never* take something of Celeste's. He'd just order his own drinks at the bars. The champagne was Celeste's and she was planning on drinking it while we cruised through Glacier Bay tomorrow."

Myrtle and Miles looked at each other. Champagne bottles were incredibly heavy. A good three or four pounds to heft.

Myrtle said softly, "Sometimes drinking can be deadly, to quote someone I know."

Miles opened his eyes wide.

Myrtle cleared her throat. "It sounds to me as if we need to start a search for your aunt. We should contact the ship's onboard security. And I should contact my son."

"Your son?" asked Eugenia in confusion.

"He's the police chief in my town. Very experienced. And he's traveling with me. But before I get him, let me just take a small look around." Myrtle knew she'd never get good evidence with Red around. If a crime *had* occurred. Which, to Myrtle, seemed very likely, with or without Wanda's prediction. Celeste also had thought her life was in danger.

The first thing that Myrtle did was to go through Celeste's closet. She felt each dress until she found one that made a crinkling sound when patted. She removed the dress, which was very simple and apparently very old, turned it inside-out, and carefully removed the pins holding the paper inside.

It was Celeste's will. And a quick reading indicated that Celeste intended on leaving everything to Eugenia. Myrtle felt a surge of smugness that she had found it.

Eugenia was still wringing her hands and looking anxious so Myrtle decided not to share this information right away. "Why don't we all go together to see my son?" she asked, glancing around the room to see if anything else provided clues to what happened. But all she saw was evidence that someone had been searching for something in the stateroom.

A couple of minutes later, they were knocking on Red's door. Elaine answered, sending them to the pool area where a late-night snack buffet was set up.

Red was taking a large bite of ice cream when he saw Myrtle, Miles, and Eugenia walking determinedly up to him. "Uh-oh," he said. "This can't be good."

Myrtle and Eugenia explained what had happened while Red listened grimly. "So you believe your aunt is missing. Based on her usual pattern of behavior."

Eugenia nodded emphatically.

Myrtle added, "And Celeste confided in me that she believed her life was in danger."

Red sighed. "Why doesn't this surprise me? Mama, you're always in the middle of everything." His expression told her that he now wanted her to have nothing more to do with this family.

Eugenia said, "I'm going to go look around the ship a bit."

As she left, Miles said in a low voice, "You know, even if it was an accident, it's not good. If she fell overboard, she'd be hitting the water very hard from such a height."

Myrtle added, "Not only that, but how cold is this water? She wouldn't be able to stand the water for very long. She'd have hypothermia."

"Let's try not to jump to conclusions," said Red in a tired voice. "Remember—the balconies outside the rooms have a pretty high railing. You have to really stand up tall to even see out. I don't think a person could accidentally fall off their stateroom balcony. Maybe she could have *jumped*, though."

Myrtle and Miles shook their heads. "Not the type," said Miles.

"Okay. Well, I guess our first order of business is to alert the ship's security officer. Then we can help with a search of the ship. Mama, you can provide any background information you might know to help us fill in the blanks after we've got the security guy with us," said Red, standing.

"We'll look around this deck so you can catch up with us when you've alerted security," said Myrtle. "And we'll catch up with Eugenia. She has a key."

But twenty minutes later when Red rejoined them, he was alone. He shook his head grimly when he walked up to them. "He's very sick and is under quarantine. I ended up speaking to him on the phone since he couldn't even answer his door."

Miles looked a little green. "What is it? Not norovirus, I hope." He glanced around for one of the hand sanitizing stations and then speedily walked to it to spritz his hands.

"No one knows what it is, but he's not in good shape. It could even be food poisoning. Regardless, they had to put him under quarantine. There's no one else. There's no provision for any type of police presence on cruise ships. He gave me the green light to do a private, informal investigation," said Red.

"Where do we start?" asked Miles. "It's a big ship. We haven't seen her on this deck, but for all we know, Celeste could be entering rooms after we leave them. Besides, with everyone out and walking around, it could be easy to miss seeing her."

Myrtle said, "We need to get back to her room. She might have returned there. Besides, her room seemed to provide some ... clues."

Red gave his mother a hard look for her obvious snooping and then said, "She's right. Back to her room first."

When they reached the stateroom, Miles said, "I'll stay outside. Not enough room for so many of us."

They walked in and Eugenia gave a shiver. "The room isn't usually like this."

"In what way?" asked Red.

"Messy. It doesn't usually have papers pulled out everywhere. And I was telling your mother that there was a champagne bottle missing. No one would touch her champagne," said Eugenia.

Red said, "Maybe *she* drank it. Did she go to a lounge, maybe, to enjoy her champagne?"

Eugenia shook her head, pushing her glasses up her nose. "No. She had plans to drink it while we were cruising through Glacier Bay. She had it this afternoon."

Red had been looking through the bits of paper. When he found the one that Myrtle recognized as the will, he stiffened and gave Eugenia a sharp look before he carefully folded the paper. "I'm going to hold onto things that I think may provide us with clues, if that's all right with you," he said smoothly.

Eugenia nodded helplessly.

Red had opened the doors to the verandah. Myrtle had already glanced outside the glass door earlier and hadn't seen anyone out on the small balcony, either sitting in one of the two chairs or sprawled on the deck.

But Red took it a step farther. He stepped into the frigid air, leaning carefully over the side, over the railing. Then he peered closer.

He stepped back in. "All the closets should have flashlights. Hand one to me, Mama."

Red took the flashlight and leaned carefully over the railing again. Then he called out to someone or something below, with no response.

He hurried in, grimly. "Can someone call the front desk? We need to get a member of the crew. Doesn't have to be security. And the ship doctor, too. There's a figure lying on top of the lifeboat tarp below."

Chapter Five

Myrtle stuck her head out the door to tell Miles.

Red gently said to Eugenia. "Why don't you go back to your room and put your feet up for a few minutes? I'll be there to fill you in shortly."

Eugenia's eyes behind her large glasses looked even more anxious and she started picking at her fingernail polish. "I should let the rest of the family know. Poor Maisy. And Terrell!" She gave a sob and put a bony fist to her mouth as if to contain any others.

Red gave Myrtle a look to indicate that he really *did* need Eugenia out of the way of a potential crime scene. "My mother will escort you back. And she'll also help track down the family."

Myrtle decided that, all in all, this wasn't a bad chore to be tasked with. After all, it would be helpful to locate the family, since they were all suspects. "It's all right, Eugenia," she said briskly. "You've had a terrible shock. Let's let you rest for a while. Don't worry about trying to round up the family. I'm happy to do that with Miles."

Eugenia obediently allowed herself to be led back to her cabin. As they passed Miles, Myrtle put up an index finger to let him know it would be a minute. When Eugenia walked into her room, she immediately plopped down on the small sofa there and burst into tears.

Myrtle, never comfortable around crying, grabbed some tissues and thrust them at Eugenia. In an effort to distract the woman, and to perhaps also provide some information for herself, Myrtle asked, "Have you *seen* the family tonight? Anyone? Have any idea where they all might be?"

Eugenia looked at her with wide eyes and then gave another sob. "They couldn't have."

"I'm not saying they did. But I wondered where everyone was," said Myrtle.

Eugenia covered her face and cried even harder. Whether this was in recognition of the fact that someone close to Celeste was most certainly behind any foul play or because she actually *did* remember something that could prove incriminating, Myrtle couldn't say.

"I'll be back soon," said Myrtle as she left the rather suffocating feel of Eugenia's stateroom. There was nothing like someone crying to make a space feel even smaller than it was.

Miles was waiting for her in the tiny hall. "The front desk is sending some crew out, as well as the ship doctor. I'm assuming they'll approach from the lower deck since they'll need to lower the lifeboat to recover the body." He paused. "I suppose it *is* a body and not someone in need of medical assistance?"

Myrtle said, "Considering the missing champagne bottle, I'm going to say it's a body. Red would want a doctor to at least pronounce the death, though, I'd imagine. But yes, it should be a body, especially keeping Wanda's dire prediction in mind."

Miles looked weary at the thought of keeping Wanda and her uncanny predictions in mind.

"The entire setup points to murder. Celeste was hit over the head with a champagne bottle and then had her body thrown over the side. She definitely didn't seem to be the suicidal type, as we mentioned before. The killer must have thought he was throwing her into the water," said Myrtle.

"He should have listened for a splash," said Miles dryly. He followed Myrtle as she started walking down the hall. "Where are we heading?"

"Red asked me to help find the family," said Myrtle.

Miles looked uncomfortable. "We'll have to tell them? That's not usually what we have to do."

"Well, it will at least help us know where everyone is. And with the security guy laid out with norovirus or whatever, we're kind of on our own," said Myrtle.

At the mention of norovirus, Miles's gaze darted around for another hand sanitizer station.

The first person they came across was Randolph. As usual, he was passed out in a chair near the piano bar with an empty glass on the floor beside him. Several passengers were gathered around a window behind Randolph, exclaiming as they looked out into the soft nighttime light. "A whale!" said one of them to Myrtle and Miles.

Randolph, however, didn't budge. A low snore emanated from him as he sat, askew, in the armchair.

Miles gently shook his arm. Again, he didn't budge.

Myrtle finally said crossly in her best schoolteacher voice, "Randolph! For heaven's sake!"

This time, his eyes opened immediately. Myrtle thought she saw a spark of recognition and sharpness there and something else before he gave them a bleary look. Was Randolph as intoxicated as he'd appeared?

Miles gave Myrtle the hopeless look of a man resigned to his fate of assisting a drunk man back to his stateroom again. He said to Randolph. "Look, we need to get you back to your room. Can you stand up and walk there yourself?"

Randolph looked at his watch. "It's very early."

"It's midnight!" said Myrtle in exasperation.

"That's what I'm saying," slurred Randolph. "That's early for someone who doesn't sleep."

"You were giving an excellent impression of sleeping a few minutes ago," observed Myrtle. "And, as a fellow insomniac, I can only advise you that you need to at least keep *trying* to sleep. Spending all night in an armchair won't do you any favors. Besides, you're needed in your cabin."

Randolph carefully stood up by propelling himself upward with both hands on the arms of the chair. He stood, wobbling a bit, before giving Myrtle and Miles a smug look and walking slowly in the direction of his room. "I can't imagine what they need me for," he muttered. "They don't usually need me."

Myrtle and Miles exchanged glances. Randolph did seem to be more lucid than he was the prior night. Actually, this might be as lucid as he got. Miles said cautiously, "It's your wife, Randolph. I'm afraid there's been an accident."

Randolph snorted. "I keep advising her to use her cane at all times. Falling down is hazardous for people her age."

Myrtle decided it might be helpful to have him go on thinking that Celeste had minor injuries. At least for the next couple of minutes. "We noticed that there was a bottle of champagne missing," she said carefully.

Randolph shook his head, a movement that apparently made it hurt because he put a hand up to his forehead. "It's nothing to do with me. I wouldn't touch her champagne. Have my own drinks and champagne gives me headaches anyway. She can't pin that on me. Must have drunk it herself and forgotten about it."

"Was it there earlier this afternoon?" asked Miles.

"Who knows!" scoffed Randolph. "*I* wasn't there earlier this afternoon. I was playing bridge."

"Or *not* playing bridge," said Myrtle wryly.

Randolph stopped his slow walking and said with great dignity, "I'm doing a good job walking, but I believe a break might be required. Perhaps in this lounge."

Myrtle sighed. At this rate, it would be breakfast before they found the rest of the family. They sat down in some red and gold upholstered chairs near large windows.

"What have you been doing this evening?" asked Myrtle.

"I'm not so much into the shows," said Randolph with a shrug. "Wasn't interested in the filming. I walked around a lot.

Checked out different bars. Obediently viewed whales when it was called for."

Myrtle narrowed her eyes, studying Randolph carefully. "As far as bridge goes, I stepped in for you when you left that game. Too restless to play, were you?"

"Perhaps I'm tired of losing to my wife," said Randolph with a short laugh.

Myrtle said, "I had a very interesting conversation with her. She's a fascinating woman."

Randolph raised his eyebrows doubtfully.

"She told me that she'd changed her will here on the ship," said Myrtle, watching closely for a reaction.

She got one, too. Randolph's eyes opened wide. Whether he was surprised that his wife had changed her will, or surprised that she had told Myrtle about it, she couldn't tell. But he said smoothly, finally, "Of course. Yes. She said she was going to do that. Naturally, I wasn't in favor of it."

"Naturally?" asked Miles.

"I assumed I might be written out of it," said Randolph with a snort. "Celeste and I haven't been seeing eye to eye lately. Well, I'll just have to spend the rest of the trip cajoling her."

Myrtle gave Miles a swift look and he shrugged. Myrtle said gently, "It was more than an accident that Celeste had. I'm afraid she's dead."

"Dead?" Randolph stared blankly at Myrtle as if Celeste couldn't possibly be dead.

"I'm sorry," she said quietly and looked anxiously at Randolph for any sign of tears.

There were no tears forthcoming, however. There was, instead, a brief calculating look before that blankness settled over him again. "Well. I'm sorry to hear that. I suppose, though, when we get older, these things are inevitable. I wish she'd been able to see Glacier Bay tomorrow, however. She was looking forward to that."

Myrtle said, "Oh, but it wasn't a natural death, you see. It wasn't her time to go. Someone murdered her."

"Have any idea who might have wanted to do that?" asked Miles solicitously.

Myrtle noticed that his eyes were lit up as if he were thinking very hard.

Myrtle repeated Miles's question and Randolph grunted. "I suppose plenty of people would," he said finally. "Although you might especially want to talk to Celeste's disgruntled son."

"The elusive Terrell?" asked Myrtle.

"That's right. He's rather antisocial," said Randolph.

"Any ideas where we might be able to find him?" asked Miles.

"Gathering cobwebs up in the library somewhere, I'm guessing," said Randolph, looking sleepy. "Reading the most boring tome in the ship or working crosswords and trying to think of a four-letter word for a French sewing case."

Miles said absently, "*Etui.*"

Myrtle gave him a reproving look and then turned back to ask Randolph more about Terrell. But Randolph appeared to be asleep, his cheek propped up on his hand. She sighed.

By the time they were able to wake Randolph, get him to stand back up, and walked back to their hall, Red was waiting for them.

"Did you take a nap?" he asked in amusement.

"No, we simply found the one who's most difficult to herd," snapped Myrtle. "Don't tell me you zipped around the ship and found the others?"

"The others wended their way back to their respective rooms with the help of the crew," said Red easily. He tilted his head a bit to one side to study Randolph, whose head was also tilted to one side. "Sir?" he asked him.

Randolph nodded and then winced a bit as if it made his head hurt.

"I'm so sorry for your loss. The cruise ship has kindly arranged for you to have another stateroom tonight. Would you like to gather a few things? It's an empty room right down the hall, so not far away," said Red.

Randolph appeared bemused, whether at the mention of any sort of loss or the mention of gathering items one might need overnight, Myrtle wasn't sure. Finally, he muttered, "I don't really need anything tonight. I'll just get some sleep." He paused, looking at Red through narrowed eyes. "You're investigating? What's the ship doing?"

Red said, "Unfortunately, I'm all we've got here in terms of investigators. Ships aren't required to have an onboard police officer, and the security person is unable to investigate."

"Have you told the others?" asked Randolph with some curiosity.

"There is a crew member here who did assist me with that as the family returned to their rooms. And they've offered the services of the ship chaplain."

Randolph grunted. "I'm okay. Is this the crew member who'll get me in the new room?" He followed the person away.

Myrtle asked, "So everyone has been informed?" It irritated her that the process of getting Randolph back to his room had taken so long.

Red walked into Celeste's stateroom and continued sorting through her things, looking for clues. "The daughter and the son have been informed. And you've spoken with the niece and the husband. I'm planning on speaking to all of them tomorrow."

"There's also a friend that Celeste was traveling with. Bettina," said Myrtle.

"Right," said Red. "I forgot to mention her. She did come by the room to ask some questions. I thought she was a shipboard friendship and not a longstanding one. I'll have to include her in the interviews tomorrow."

Myrtle said, "I know you're looking for clues, but I think the *biggest* one has already been found. By me. The will should help us cement a good motive for Celeste's death. You may not realize, but it wasn't simply lying out on her desk or bed. It was pinned in one of her everyday dresses and I found it."

Red rolled his eyes. "I can tell that we're not going to be able to move forward until I congratulate you on your discovery. Good sleuthing, although I have no idea why you were searching for a will to begin with and I'm not sure I want to know. As of this minute, I want you to *stop* with the sleuthing, Mama. It's going to get you into trouble—or maybe even killed. There's someone who means business on this ship."

Myrtle was about to respond hotly when Miles interrupted. "Did the crew ... well, what have they done with Celeste's body?"

"And were you able to get any additional information about what might have happened to her?" asked Myrtle.

Red said, "Oh, the ship is outfitted with its own morgue."

Myrtle and Miles just stared at him.

"It's not all that surprising, if you think about it, y'all. It's not for murder victims, it's for natural deaths," said Red. "Think of their clientele."

Myrtle said grudgingly, "I suppose the average passenger age is somewhat ... elevated."

"Exactly. So they have a spot for Celeste and she will be safely there until we return," said Red.

Miles said, "Then the local police will do an autopsy and investigate?"

Red raised a finger. "Ah! Yes, that's what one would think. However, it's not actually the case. If a murder or any suspicious death takes place in international waters, the cruise line is allowed to handle the investigation."

"And how do they do *that*?" asked Myrtle, hands on her hips.

"Poorly. It's handled by lawyers and generally swept under the rug as much as possible. The cruise line's risk management lawyers take care of it on the shore ... never even setting foot on the ship," said Red.

Miles asked, "And perhaps there's a bit of hush money or a financial settlement of some kind here and there?"

"I'm guessing in some cases, yes. And heaven forbid if a crew member is potentially involved in a death. There's absolutely no follow-up at all there. Why would there be? It's in the ship's best interest to forgive and forget," said Red. "To cover up. Remind me never to get murdered at sea."

Myrtle frowned. "Wait. But you're not saying that a crew member is possibly behind this."

"No, I'm not, because that's pretty unlikely. It's most likely that it's one of Celeste's entourage of family and friends. They had the most to gain, or thought they did," said Red, glancing around the small stateroom at the paper clutter.

Myrtle said, "You're talking about the will. That I found."

"Why do I have the feeling you're going to explain how you knew there was a will in her cabin?" asked Red in a tired voice.

"Celeste was talking about it to me," said Myrtle. "She also mentioned that she thought her life was in danger."

"Well, if she went around telling people she was changing her will and unscrupulous people thought they might get cut out, then of course, her life was in danger," said Red with a sigh. "But all of this can be dealt with tomorrow. The ship has changed the lock on the stateroom and I've got access. It's time to get a bit of sleep and look at it all again tomorrow."

Myrtle said thoughtfully, "I suppose there will be a panic onboard, won't there?"

"A panic?" asked Red in a distracted voice.

"Certainly. Once the passengers realize that there was a murder on the ship, there's bound to be complete pandemonium. Think of it—it's just like one of those country house murders, isn't it? A closed off location with a limited number of suspects?" asked Myrtle.

"Limited?" asked Red dryly. "On the contrary, this ship is so big that it's got a higher population than our hometown. There are roughly five thousand people onboard."

"Whatever. You know what I mean," said Myrtle.

"I do and *no*. There will be no panic or pandemonium. That's because no one is going to tell anyone about the murder. The family wants it under wraps and so does the ship. I was specifically asked not to say anything about it," said Red pointedly. "And you shouldn't mention it either."

Miles cleared his throat. "Did they find out what happened?"

"To Celeste? Well, it was just the ship doctor, a Dr. Powers, that I talked to, but when I briefly observed her body during recovery—definitely blunt force trauma with a heavy object. The killer must have supposed he was getting rid of the evidence by chucking everything over the side. But there was a handy lifeboat jutting out a bit," said Red.

Miles nodded. "That's good to know, of course. I meant though, if you knew what happened to the *security* man."

Red stared blankly at Miles and a smile started playing around Myrtle's lips at Miles's germphobia.

Miles continued, "You know—was it norovirus? Or just food poisoning? Because if it were food poisoning, it's not contagious. Norovirus, on the other hand?" Miles shuddered.

Red's eyes twinkled and he said, "I'm not sure, and I don't even know if there's a really good way for the ship to diagnose it. But I do know he and his germs are in quarantine for seventy-two hours after he's symptom-free, so you should be in good shape." He gave a tremendous yawn, which had the domino effect of making Myrtle and Miles yawn, too. He stood up and pointedly looked at the door to the hall.

Myrtle and Miles obediently stood up and walked out. Red said sternly to his mother, "Now, Mama, I have no doubt this episode has tweaked your interest. But remember—you're on vacation. You shouldn't have an opportunity in the world to be bored enough to try to poke around in this case. The only reason *I'm* doing it is from a sense of obligation to my occupation—and a real dislike of hearing that lawyers would be handling the investigation. You just sit back and enjoy Glacier Bay, all right?"

"Of *course*, Red. I'm here for the bears and the salmon, not to investigate murders!" said Myrtle indignantly.

But Miles gave her a long-suffering, knowing look as they headed off for their separate staterooms.

Chapter Six

Despite the late hour she'd turned in, Myrtle set an alarm to get up extremely early. It was the day they were going through Glacier Bay and she'd heard that you had to be up and about early to get a decent window seat on the ship.

She was sure that Miles would also want a good seat so she tapped on his stateroom door. And tapped again. A few minutes later, quite a few minutes, a bleary-eyed Miles opened the door.

"Sleeping?" asked Myrtle, surprised. "What about the glaciers?"

Miles disappeared for a moment and returned to thrust a jacket at Myrtle.

"What's this for?" Myrtle demanded.

"It's my stand-in," said Miles.

"You want me to reserve you a seat with your jacket? That's hardly fair, is it?" asked Myrtle.

"I think it's only unfair when one is reserving three or more," said Miles. "Fewer than three is completely fair and even desirable. Especially when one is trying to catch up on sleep."

"Is your stand-in any good at investigating murder?" asked Myrtle.

But Miles was already stumbling back into his room.

Myrtle grumbled under her breath. Then she quickly smiled as she spotted their cabin steward. Perhaps he was also Celeste's steward and had seen something unusual last night.

"Arvin?" she asked.

"Good morning," he said cheerfully as he carefully placed a list of daily activities in the slot beside each cabin door. "Need some help?"

"I do, yes. I suppose you know about the tragedy that happened last night," said Myrtle briskly.

But the mention of the tragedy seemed to make Arvin very uncomfortable. He looked away and his bright smile faded a little. "Not much. I don't know much about that," he said. A wrinkle of concern lined his forehead.

It appeared the ship was already in the process of ensuring there was no bad publicity resulting from Celeste's death. How tiresome. "You don't really have to know much about it, Arvin, I only want to know if you saw or heard anything unusual last night."

Now he did look her directly in the eye. "Nothing. I saw nothing, madam. I knock on the door to turn down the bed and the lady tells me *not now*."

Myrtle said, "So you *were* the steward for the lady who died?"

Arvin appeared very uncomfortable again at the mention of *death*, but nodded. "I was the steward for her, yes. And I saw and heard nothing."

"All right. Thank you, Arvin," said Myrtle, disappointed.

"Okay to clean, madam?" he asked.

"Oh, yes, certainly. I'll be out for a while," said Myrtle.

Myrtle proceeded to the upper level which housed a library, a bar, a coffee and croissant counter, and quite a few comfortable seats. The entire floor was lined with windows and Myrtle appeared to have the pick of them all. The only other person up there, besides staff, was a bespectacled man with a neatly trimmed goatee who was hunched over a newspaper.

Myrtle put her cardigan and Miles's jacket on two seats with good views and then curiously walked up to the man with the newspaper. He glanced up at her but didn't acknowledge her before continuing his work on the crossword puzzle in front of him. He certainly seemed to fit the description of Terrell.

Myrtle cleared her throat, and this time Terrell sat up straighter and looked her in the eye.

"Excuse me," she said, "but, are you Terrell?"

He sighed as if being Terrell was actually a tremendous burden he bore. "I'm afraid so. What's wrong?"

"Wrong? Oh ... for me? Nothing is wrong. Why would you think so?" asked Myrtle.

"Only because whenever anyone on a trip has an ingrown toenail or an abdominal pain of any description, my dear mother instructs them to find me. Since I'm a physician," said Terrell.

Myrtle said, "No. Nothing is wrong with me. But ... your mother ... I suppose the staff found you last night? I was helping the crew inform the family."

Terrell pressed his lips into a thin line. "Are you trying to ask whether I know my mother has passed on into the hereafter? I'm aware, yes."

Myrtle just stared at him. Surely he should at least *pretend* he was sad about the death of his mother? At least to a perfect stranger.

He sighed. "I suppose you think that I ought to be exhibiting more grief at her demise. I can only say that, as a physician, I'm rather inured to death. Death happens a lot and it's quite natural."

"Maybe that's true," said Myrtle. "But nothing about this death was natural."

"Still. She was an old woman," said Terrell.

"Who was looking forward to seeing Glacier Bay today!" said Myrtle sharply. "Which apparently you couldn't possibly care less about seeing as how you've buried yourself in a crossword puzzle as we go past a national treasure."

Terrell shrugged. "We have eight hours of icy fjords. I'm sure I'll catch a glimpse."

"Is this where you were last night, too?" asked Myrtle.

"Last night, not being able to abide everyone's excitement at being on film, I turned in early. So I was in my room whenever the excitement began," said Terrell.

"Alone?" asked Myrtle.

"I'm unaccompanied on this trip," said Terrell coolly.

Myrtle frowned. "But I understood that none of the family were available in their rooms when the crew tried to alert them."

"I'm a hard sleeper. Eventually, I did wake up. You can ask the crew—I wasn't rounded up from any far-flung parts of the ship. I was in my room."

His room was likely very close to his mother's too, since she would have done all the ticket purchasing at once, presumably. It would have been very easy for him to slip back unnoticed after murdering her. "Have you any idea who might have done something like this?"

Terrell was already becoming absorbed in his crossword puzzle again. "Everyone. She wasn't exactly beloved."

"That's rather facetious," said Myrtle in a scolding tone. "Surely someone in your party showed some signs that they were at a breaking point with your mother. A clue of some sort."

Terrell stared at her. "Who are you, Miss Marple or something?"

"Don't be silly. I'm far older than Miss Marple," snapped Myrtle.

Terrell looked at her with something approaching respect. Then he reflected for a couple of moments. "I would say that Randolph is the most likely candidate as the killer, then. If I had to pick and choose."

"Really?" asked Myrtle, raising her eyebrows.

"It was my pick, remember? And he's my pick. You doubt his capability?" asked Terrell.

"Frankly? Yes. Although I recognize that I might be prejudiced by the fact that I've only seen him roaring drunk. On the occasions that I've interacted with Randolph, I think it more likely that your *mother* would have picked *him* up and thrown him off the verandah," said Myrtle. "What makes you think he could have done it?"

Terrell said idly, while gazing at the puzzle, "Several things. For one, I'm not sure he's always drunk. I'm fairly certain that sometimes he's taking everything in and his intoxication is a handy façade. Besides that, he believed he was going to inherit my mother's estate."

"And this estate ... is significant?" asked Myrtle. Despite what Celeste's friend Bettina said, Myrtle was still trying to wrap her head around the fact that Celeste, who didn't look as if she had two dimes to rub together, was wealthy.

"Yes. Randolph is a leech. He believed he'd inherit Mother's fortune, got tired of waiting for her to expire naturally, and decided to speed things up a little bit," said Terrell.

Myrtle said in a somewhat smug voice, "By the way, I found your mother's will. She'd cleverly hidden it away, but I was able to discover it."

"So I have *you* to blame," said Terrell, giving her an increasingly annoyed look.

Myrtle decided to move on since Terrell didn't appear to be in the mood to compliment her sleuthing skills. "Speaking of Randolph, what exactly does he *do*?"

"He does nothing," said Terrell emphatically.

"What would he be doing if he weren't leeching off your mother, then?" asked Myrtle.

"He's allegedly an engineer," said Terrell. "Although I haven't seen evidence of the kind of intellect necessary to become one."

"So you believe that he had a financial motive for murder. Although the will changed," said Myrtle. "And he was cut out of it."

"Weren't we all?" said Terrell dryly.

"You've *seen* the will?" asked Myrtle. Considering it was pinned on the inside of a dress, this seemed extremely unlikely.

"I'm merely assuming. Mother was always threatening me with writing me out of the will. I'm expecting that if she actually *decided* to make another document, she went through with it.

When she became serious about something, she wasn't the kind of person to issue idle threats," said Terrell. He glanced around. "If you care about the glaciers as much as it seems you do, you should likely defend your territory."

It was definitely filling up. Myrtle stood up. She studied Terrell's puzzle through narrowed eyes. There was one that was quite obviously left blank in the middle of the crossword. "Your answer there is *erato*," she said briskly, giving the evil eye to a passenger who appeared to be encroaching on her chosen seats.

"Pardon?" asked Terrell.

"For the clue *sister of Clio*," said Myrtle impatiently.

"Yes, of course," said Terrell. "I just hadn't gotten to that one yet."

As Myrtle hurried away to her seat, she smiled grimly to herself. Terrell wasn't as smart as he thought himself to be. She could tell he was a very methodical puzzler and had skipped that clue because he didn't know it. *Erato* was a very common answer in puzzles—known as a repeater. If Terrell could lie about his crosswords, he could lie about anything. And despite his superior attitude, Myrtle knew she could outwit him.

Ten minutes later, a grouchy-looking Miles sat next to her with a large coffee.

"Oh good, you're up," said Myrtle.

Miles's eyes were at half-mast. He tried to drink the coffee but winced and carefully removed the lid to let it cool a bit. "Any news?" he croaked.

"News? You mean besides the fact that Terrell is *not* the smarty pants he thinks he is?" said Myrtle, chortling.

Miles gazed levelly at her. "I have no idea what that means or why it's important. Who is Terrell again?"

"Celeste's son. He's a physician and definitely not a fan of his late mother's. We need to discover why," said Myrtle in a musing tone.

"Can't we just ask him?" asked Miles. He tried to take another sip from his coffee and his eyes opened wide with alarm at its temperature. Surreptitiously, he redeposited the sip back into the cup.

"Not recommended. He's hardly the most forthcoming person I've ever met. No, I think we need to ask somebody else. Bettina seemed pretty gossipy. Maybe we can also work to get Randolph's opinion of his stepson," said Myrtle.

"How do you propose we do that? Randolph is three sheets to the wind most of the time," said Miles.

"Or is he? I've gotten the impression from my own observations and from what Terrell told me that Randolph may be taking in a lot more than he's letting on. That he might be faking some of the drunkenness. But I was thinking that maybe *you* could talk with Randolph again. He might let his guard down with you. He's retired, just like you are. Even though he's a retired engineer, you should still have a lot in common to talk about. Business is business, after all. Engineering and insurance work couldn't be that far apart." Myrtle craned her neck as someone nearby excitedly said they'd seen a whale breach.

Miles stared coldly at her.

"For heaven's sake, Miles, whatever is wrong? I don't have the time to tiptoe around your delicate ego," said Myrtle.

"Insurance has *nothing* to do with engineering," said Miles.

"If you say so," said Myrtle with a shrug.

"Although fortunately, that doesn't matter, since I was an *engineer*," said Miles.

"Were you?" asked Myrtle vaguely. She glanced over at Miles and sighed. "Grinding your teeth is bad for you, you know."

Miles pressed his lips closed as if preventing words from recklessly flying out.

Suddenly a small body launched itself at Myrtle's legs. "Jack!" she said in delight. "You're awake."

"Ohhh yes," said Elaine dryly. "He's awake all right. Has been for a while now. At this rate, though, he'll peter out for a nice afternoon nap."

Myrtle stood up and gingerly picked up Jack to let him stand on her seat. "See that, Jack? Look on the rocks there. Those white specks are mountain goats!"

"Are they?" asked Elaine.

"According to the people yelling on the other side of the lounge, they are," said Myrtle. "And you might just get to see a humpback whale that's been following alongside the ship."

Jack jumped up and down on the seat and Elaine quickly removed him and held his hand tightly. "Jack and I are going to get a nice breakfast. Preferably one with no sugar in it whatsoever."

Miles smiled and took another cautious sip of his coffee. He winced again.

"Were you able to get any sleep last night, what with Red being out late and Jack getting up early?" asked Myrtle.

Elaine shrugged. "Here and there I slept. Jack and I will both probably turn in early tonight. Red might, too. Out late and up early."

Myrtle frowned. "I haven't seen Red yet. Has he even gotten his breakfast?"

"That I don't know. I saw him out on the bow of the ship talking to one of the family or someone," said Elaine.

Miles said, "Can you describe her?"

"Attractive older woman sporting a tan and wearing lots of colorful jewelry," said Elaine.

"Bettina," chorused Myrtle and Miles.

Jack started jogging away from them and Elaine heaved a sigh. "See you later," she called behind her.

Myrtle said, "Now we have a mission."

"Have we?" asked Miles dubiously.

"We can talk to Bettina out on the bow," said Myrtle, gathering up her sweater.

"Won't it be very cold?" asked Miles. "And won't we lose the seats that you saved for us?"

"It's not supposed to be so bad out there. Besides, we will get a much better view from the bow. Unobstructed."

Miles still seemed wishy-washy and Myrtle quickly added, "We can leave the sweater and your coat here. No one will want them. We won't be long. And it will be the perfect opportunity to finally cool off your coffee once and for all. What on earth did they pour into that cup? Scalding water?"

Miles sighed, but as if realizing there was no point in trying to argue, he carefully arranged his jacket on the chair, held tightly to his coffee cup, and followed Myrtle.

It was, in fact, not nearly as cold outside as you might think Glacier Bay *should* be. But it was chilly enough to need a light jacket or sweater. Myrtle frowned as they walked onto the bow of the ship. "Wee bit nippy," she said absently.

Miles rolled his eyes.

Bettina was easy to spot. As usual, she was dressed nicely and wearing full makeup and jewelry. When she spotted Myrtle, she gave a small wave and then gave Miles a spontaneous hug that startled him, nearly making him drop his coffee cup.

"Isn't this amazing?" Bettina demanded. "Every once in a while a large piece drops off with a tremendous splash in the water. Spectacular."

Myrtle noticed that Bettina didn't lead with talking about Celeste. But then, as far as Bettina knew, Myrtle knew nothing about the incident.

"It's certainly amazing. There was quite a bit of excitement in the lounge over humpback whale spottings, too. Although the people in the lounge also get excited over moose and we see moose all the time," said Myrtle.

"Did you have fun last night?" asked Bettina abruptly.

Myrtle and Miles glanced at each other. Myrtle suspected she wasn't referring to their body discovering and family notifying activities, but to the filming that Bettina had been so excited about during the bridge game.

Myrtle said, "The filming? It was fun at first. And it was especially fun to see the actors in between scenes—when they were just real people. But it got somewhat tedious after a while and we left."

Bettina nodded. "I know just what you mean, although I did decide to stay for the whole thing. I wasn't ready to turn in yet and stayed because there was no other real entertainment that I was interested in. I thought Samuel Kingston did a nice job with his part, but I really think he does a better job when he's acting for *Tomorrow's Promise*. Maybe he needs to stick with soaps."

Miles, who had become quite a fan of the soap, agreed. "He was in over his head with this role." He took a hesitant sip of his coffee and then a large gulp. It had finally, and dramatically, cooled off.

Myrtle said, "I think our early departure from the filming was why we found out about the tragic death of your friend."

Bettina blinked at Myrtle in surprise.

Myrtle continued, "So after you finished being an extra, is that when the ship's crew notified you about Celeste?"

Bettina nodded. "I didn't think you knew and I hated having a serious conversation in such a gorgeous place. But yes, that's when I learned the news. Absolutely horrible. Poor, dear Celeste. Clearly, she booked and paid for a ticket for her own killer. It's just wrong."

Myrtle said, hugging her body with her arms as a chilly breeze blew by, "So you believe that she was murdered by someone close to her."

Bettina raised her carefully penciled eyebrows. "Of course I do. I haven't heard any suggestion that she wasn't. It's hardly plausible that a band of ruffians attacked her and threw her over the side. Why would they?"

"You'd mentioned at the bridge game yesterday that Celeste had a challenging relationship with her family," said Myrtle.

"That's one way of putting it. She did bring some of it on herself. Celeste was fond of games of all sorts and she was very good at them," said Bettina.

"I'll say," muttered Miles, still smarting from his loss at bridge the day before.

Myrtle leaned against the side of the ship as the wind buffeted her a bit. "Celeste manipulated people, is that it?"

"She was a master manipulator," said Bettina. "She could make anyone do anything."

Miles said curiously, "You either control your feelings really well or else you're not all that upset over your friend's death. Which surprises me since it was so sudden and so violent."

Bettina sighed and batted her lashes at Miles, making him squirm uncomfortably. "That must make me seem awful. But the truth is that I'm *not* really all that surprised. Celeste has been deliberately pushing everyone's buttons for the entire trip. She's been talking about revamping her will, haranguing her children, bossing her niece. Celeste has been completely incorrigible and everyone has been getting more and more agitated about it. So was her death a surprise? Yes and no."

"Who do you think is most likely to have been responsible for her death?" asked Myrtle.

"Does it matter?" asked Bettina with a shrug. "From what I understand from the policeman who's investigating, the ship couldn't possibly care less. The ... *investigation* ... for lack of a better word, will be conducted by a bunch of risk-adverse lawyers on the shore and quickly hushed up."

Myrtle cleared her throat. "The policeman, just FYI, is my son. I do believe he'll find out as much information as possible, only because he believes wrongdoing must be punished. I'm not sure what the cruise line will do with the information once they have it. But yes, I still believe it's important. I feel we owe it to Celeste to find out who's behind this."

Bettina thought about this before nodding. "I can see that. That's quite noble of you, really. In that case ... Eugenia did it. Naturally."

Miles said quickly, "Really? Is that what you think? That little quiet girl?"

Bettina frowned at him. "Certainly. Celeste has been bullying her nonstop. She's been bullying her nonstop for *years*. And she's hardly a little girl. She's thirty if she's a day."

"What do you know about Eugenia?" asked Myrtle curiously. "You've been acquainted with the family for a while, haven't you?"

"I have," said Bettina. "I've known Celeste since we were in school together. And I've known Eugenia since she started helping out Celeste."

"How long has Eugenia been helping?" asked Myrtle.

"And why did Celeste *choose* Eugenia to begin with? She seemed very irritated with her from what I could tell," said Miles.

"Celeste chose Eugenia because she would do whatever she wanted her to do. She'd tried having real nurses, but they were too bossy and Celeste hated them. She hired Eugenia several years ago. She was, as you so astutely noticed, Miles, very annoyed with what she saw as Eugenia's shortcomings. But, in general, she saw Eugenia as a good solution."

"Why did she even *need* a nurse?" asked Myrtle. "She seemed fine to me."

"She's had recurrent bouts of rheumatoid arthritis. Different medications provide different results. Sometimes it would flare up and Celeste would need more help than others," said Bettina.

Myrtle paused with her questions while a fellow tourist asked Bettina to take her photo with the glaciers as a backdrop.

"Sorry," said Bettina, after she'd taken a few shots for the tourist, "What was I saying?"

"Eugenia," prompted Miles.

"You were giving us background," said Myrtle. "We understand she was Celeste's niece?"

"That's right. Her first husband's sister's child. He died decades ago, but Celeste was still connected with the family. Eugenia is basically the poor relation. Her family farmed her out to Celeste, likely hoping to stay in her good graces and perhaps benefit from the will that Celeste was so fond of throwing in everyone's face." Bettina looked reflective. "Actually, this would make a fantastic episode for *Tomorrow's Promise*."

"Or a Bronte or Austen novel," muttered Myrtle.

Miles said, "Does Eugenia have ... well ... a *life* at all? Was she constantly at the beck and call of Celeste's whims, or did she have time off to do fun stuff?"

Bettina snorted. "I'm not sure that Eugenia would know how to do 'fun stuff' if she tried. She's not exactly gifted socially. And wouldn't I love to get my hands on her for a makeover? I'd take a lot more advantage of my looks if I were her age again."

Myrtle didn't doubt it. She said, "But you still think that Eugenia has the best motive for murder? Even though she apparently wouldn't feel shortchanged by her lack of free time?"

"It's not the lack of free time. It's the bullying. And not just that—she had a *huge* financial motive," said Bettina.

Myrtle raised her eyebrows. "You know about the new will?"

"Well, I knew what Celeste told me. She could have been making idle threats about changing her will and writing everyone out of it. But idle or not, Eugenia overheard her talking about it when Celeste and I were waiting in line for dinner. The girl's face was bright red—poor child has no poker face whatsoever. Of *course* she's a prime suspect. And she would have had plenty of opportunity to do it. Think of it! Everyone else was scurrying around the ship, listening to piano players, watching the filming, or getting plastered at various bars. Eugenia was simply in and out of Celeste's room all the time!"

Myrtle said, "The more I hear about Celeste, the more demanding and unpleasant she sounds. But you liked her." The last sentence came out more as a question.

"Sure I did. She was wicked smart and funny. She could be *difficult*, but ultimately, she was a good person at heart," said Bettina. "And now, if you'll excuse me, I'm absolutely freezing. I'm going to have to head in and warm up for a while before I come back out again." She gave them a quick smile and hurried back in, throwing over her shoulder, "Maybe we can put together another bridge game. We have a much better chance of winning now that Celeste's not around." She winked at Miles and gave him a little wave as she left.

Myrtle and Miles stared after her.

Chapter Seven

"She doesn't sound particularly heartbroken, does she?" mused Myrtle.

"She's a very matter-of-fact person," said Miles. "And rather a flirtatious one, too." He carefully poured the remainder of his coffee cup's contents over the side of the ship.

"Miles! Ditching your coffee after all your nursing of it?" asked Myrtle incredulously.

"Now it's too cold to drink," said Miles. "Which is understandable, considering your lips are turning a very distinct color of blue. And I doubt that's the shade of your lipstick."

"All right, all right, we're heading back inside. But, really, Miles. You sound like Goldilocks with all this 'too hot and too cold' nonsense."

They walked back into the ship and to their saved spots. A couple of passengers who were standing around and trying to peer out the windows gave them baleful looks for the reserved seats.

"Our popularity soars," murmured Miles.

"They're just jealous! Let *them* get up at dawn and save seats if they want the best view," said Myrtle.

"Is there even a dawn when it's light all night?" asked Miles.

Before Myrtle could respond with her thoughts on the issue, she noticed that a birdlike woman with bright blue eyes was approaching them with great determination. "Do you know this woman, Miles?" she muttered.

"No. Should I?" asked Miles.

"She sure seems to know us," said Myrtle. "And I have a bad feeling about it. I somehow sense Red's interference."

"You're being silly. She's probably going to ask us where the restrooms are or something," said Miles. "You always seem to suspect poor Red."

"For good reason," said Myrtle with a sniff.

The small woman said in a triumphant voice, "You must be Myrtle Clover!"

"My fame precedes me, I see," said Myrtle dryly. "Or have we met?"

"Your son described you to me in such vivid detail that I knew you on the spot," said the woman.

Myrtle shot Miles a look and he shrugged.

"I won't ask what adjectives Red used to describe me," drawled Myrtle. "You needed to find me for some reason?"

"Yes. Your son says that you're quite the experienced reader. And a *teacher*, I believe, right?" asked the woman. "I'm Violet, by the way."

"I suppose once a teacher, always a teacher," said Myrtle with a sigh. "Is there something that you needed taught? I'm on vacation, you see."

Violet gave a tinkling laugh. "Oh no, nothing like that. It's only that I'd find your insights interesting. You see, I've formed a small book club and Red said that you'd be a wonderful candidate for it."

Myrtle gritted her teeth. Red's attempts to control her were bad enough on dry land. To do it on the high seas while she was on vacation was insufferable.

Miles eyed Myrtle warily in case she exploded.

Myrtle took a deep, steadying breath. "Very thoughtful of him. But there are so many activities that I can't imagine possibly fitting a book club in."

Miles added, "Besides, I've taken a look at the ship library. They may have more than one copy of a title, but no more than that."

"You must be Miles," said the woman with a smile. "Red described you, too."

Miles looked a bit anxious upon hearing this. He'd be fretting, wondering how Red described him.

"But to answer your question, this is a book club like no other. It's quite extraordinary," said Violet.

"Meaning you're discussing real literary works?" asked Miles hopefully. He was always up for a good discussion on Alexandre Dumas or Dostoyevsky. It was just so rare that he could find a willing partner to engage in this activity.

Myrtle tilted her head skeptically. Violet didn't look like a scholar.

Again Violet gave her tinkling laugh. "Heavens, no! As you stated Myrtle, we're on *vacation*. So our group is going to discuss our favorite *fun* books of all time. It will be a roundtable discussion. We'll be meeting each day at lunch near the buffet— at noon, exactly. I'll be the timekeeper and ensure we don't run a hair over our allotted time of twenty minutes."

Myrtle said, "*Fun* books."

"That's right. So you and Miles join us and be sure to bring a pen and paper so that you can list all the wonderful books that the book club members recommend. It will be *stimulating!*"

Violet disappeared as quickly as she'd arrived.

Miles said, "I guess Red is trying to fill up your time so you won't be able to do any investigating."

"That Red! As if he can stop me. *Fun* books. The very idea!" said Myrtle indignantly.

"What's your idea of a fun book?" asked Miles curiously.

"A collection of short stories by Eudora Welty. What about you?"

Miles said thoughtfully, "Maybe a classic adventure story? *On the Road* by Jack Kerouac? Something like that?"

"You and I would be banned from their book club," said Myrtle decidedly. "I have a feeling their discussion will be populated by celebrity memoirs."

They resumed their viewing of Glacier Bay for a good ten to fifteen minutes. The glaciers were icily gorgeous. "We're definitely not in Bradley anymore," said Miles. "So who is next on our interviewing list? Celeste's partying daughter? Her long-suffering, angelic niece? Or do we have another go at her no-good husband since he was hardly coherent when we last spoke with him?"

"I'd rather speak with Eugenia first. But if we spot the elusive Maisy, I guess we could grab the opportunity. Eugenia is fresh in my mind since Bettina was going on about her so much," said Myrtle.

"Eugenia, from what I gather, doesn't seem like the kind to be out and about much," said Miles doubtfully.

"Maybe that *was* true. But now Eugenia is free of Celeste. And, from what we can tell, she's quite the heiress. Who knows ... maybe her behavior will change?" Myrtle shrugged.

But they didn't see Eugenia. Not at lunch or in any of the observation lounges they visited.

Myrtle and Miles were leaving dinner from the main dining room, feeling stuffed and sleepy as usual, when they heard a raucous laughing. A loud voice said, "No, *really*. Drinks are on me! I've got reason to celebrate!"

The woman and her companion, a tall man with long hair pulled back in a ponytail, came into view. Her hair was dyed a platinum blonde and she wore a low-cut top, a lot of makeup, and was tottering around on very high heels.

The man with the ponytail sounded amused. "Are you sure about that? You just lost your mother. That's hardly reason for a party."

"You didn't know my mother," said the woman, with a shrug. "I'm going to have a seat. Can you round up a waiter or a wine steward or someone and order us some vodka tonics? I'll be right here to sign the check to bill it to my room."

Myrtle whispered, "We've sighted our Maisy. Come on."

"Another intoxicated suspect?" murmured Miles with a resigned sigh.

"I don't think she is, no. She's just in high spirits. And I want to find out why," said Myrtle, stepping carefully and leaning on her cane as the ship rolled a bit. Miles fingered the acupressure band on his wrist.

"Excuse me," said Myrtle in her best trembling old lady voice, "are you Maisy, dear?"

Myrtle sat down next to Maisy on the small settee that was against the wall of the hall leading to the dining room.

Maisy gave her an ambivalent look out of eyes heavily encrusted with dark eyeshadow, and regarded Miles similarly. "I am. Sorry, do I know you?"

"I'm Myrtle Clover and this is my friend Miles Bradford. We'd become acquainted with your mother during this cruise."

Maisy gave a short, snorting laugh. "I'm so very sorry to hear that. My condolences."

Myrtle said coolly, "Interesting. I was just about to say the same to you. Offer my condolences, I mean. I was sorry to learn of your mother's death. Celeste was a very interesting woman."

"That's one way of putting it. I appreciate your thoughtfulness, but believe me, I'm doing just fine," said Maisy.

Miles said delicately, "You and your mother weren't particularly close?"

"Close? Well, if you're talking about *physically* close, then yes, we were close. Close enough for me to feel completely suffocated by her. Were we *emotionally* close? No." Maisy fished out one of the ice cubes from her empty glass and put it in her mouth. She started emphatically crunching the ice, a sound which made Miles wince.

Myrtle said, "Celeste was ... controlling, then?"

"She was a control *freak*, that's what she was. She didn't stop at 'controlling.' She wanted to be the puppeteer and manipulate everyone to do what she wanted them to do. And now she's gone. I can't pretend to be sad about that. I'm doing all the things that I always wanted to do. Dancing, drinking, having the time of my life. Mother and I were already arguing before she died. That's because I'd already decided that, for this cruise anyway, I was going to have fun. She *hated* seeing me enjoy myself. She hated the clothes I bought for this trip and the makeup I was wearing. And she didn't like that I started seeing one of the passengers."

Myrtle nodded. "Miles and I were actually dispatched to help find the family when your mother's death was discovered. I'm guessing, from what you've been saying, that you were out and about on the ship during that time?"

Maisy's mouth pursed in a cupid's smile. "Oh, so you're one of the helpful team of amateurs who has taken it upon themselves to investigate, is that right?"

Myrtle bristled a bit at *amateurs*. "A gifted amateur, with some past experience in investigations of this sort. Miles is experienced, too."

Miles, unfortunately, took that opportunity to drop the rolls he had taken from the dining room on the floor. Myrtle sighed and Maisy appeared to be suppressing a grin.

"At any rate, my son, who is a police chief, is certainly *not* an amateur, gifted or otherwise. I am helping him out," said Myrtle.

"Right. Well, to answer your question, I was out. Guy and I were at the piano bar, as a matter of fact. We were trying our hand at accompanying the piano," said Maisy.

Miles, who had recovered and tossed the errant rolls into a nearby receptacle, returned to overhear the last bit. "Accompanying it? With ... what? A cello?"

Maisy looked amused again. "No, silly. Does anyone travel with a cello? With our *voices*. Sort of a karaoke. Without the words. Sometimes we made up the words."

Miles appeared pained at this information. Myrtle had the feeling that the pianist had, too.

"To me, the saddest part of this whole thing is that your mother's death wasn't natural," said Myrtle. "It's very hard to believe she was murdered."

Maisy raised her eyebrows archly. "Absolutely not. It's definitely *not* hard to believe she was murdered. I'd have murdered her myself if I'd been creative enough to figure out a way of doing it. Kudos to the murderer for finding a means— that's got to be challenging on a ship. We have to go through so much security to get here that it's got to be almost impossible to put one's hands on a weapon."

Miles cleared his throat. "I suppose you know it was a champagne bottle. Very heavy, of course."

Maisy nodded. "Yes. And ironic that alcohol would, even indirectly, kill Mother. She wasn't much of a drinker." She glanced at her watch. "Speaking of, where did Guy get to with those drinks?"

"You say that you can easily see that someone would have murdered your mother. Why? And who do you think is most likely?" asked Myrtle.

Maisy gave that snorting laugh again. "Who *didn't* want to? Mother stifled me. She bossed Eugenia. She was a horrid friend to Bettina. She belittled Randolph. And she ruined Terrell's life. Out of all those people and all the potential motives? It's hard to say."

"Your mother ruined Terrell's life?" asked Miles politely. "Does that still happen in this day and age? Young people are too independent to allow their parents to interfere with their lives enough to ruin them."

"Terrell was under Mother's thumb when he was a teenager. He didn't have an original thought in that egghead of his," said Maisy. "I felt sorry for him."

"What did your mother push him into?" asked Myrtle.

"What *didn't* she push him into?" asked Maisy. "She forced him to go to med school, forced him to get married to someone completely unsuited for him. He ended up in a profession he despises and is divorced all because Mother wanted the prestige of having a son in medicine."

Miles said, "But Terrell is a middle-aged man. Surely any bitterness from being pushed into medicine and marriage must be long gone?"

Maisy raised her eyebrows. "Clearly, you don't know Terrell. He's the definition of the word *bitter*. He's convinced he could have been an astronaut or some such nonsense. He always was very interested in science as a kid, but not biology. His thing was space. All he does is mope around all day and shoot Mother hateful looks. What's more, I heard him having a huge argument with her just a couple of days ago."

"What did he say?" asked Myrtle.

"Well, as I overheard, he was barely able to get a word in edgewise because Mother was really letting him have it. You see, for her, *Terrell* was letting *her* down, not the other way around. The only thing I heard him say back was in this really cold voice of his: *you'll be sorry*."

Myrtle and Miles glanced at each other. That did indeed sound ominous.

Maisy suddenly studied them through narrow eyes. "Say. Do you two like to dance?"

Myrtle laughed. "I never was crazy about it and now I'm definitely out of practice. Why?"

"The dancing on the ship in the disco room is really fun," said Maisy. "And the more people the better—it really makes it more exciting when the room is crowded." She could apparently tell that Myrtle and Miles were not very enthusiastic about the disco room. "Sometimes they play slower stuff, too. You should try it out."

Miles said, "Actually, the idea of the ship moving and me moving that fast and a disco ball throwing lights up on the wall ... it's making me feel a little nauseated." He pushed the band on his wrist.

Maisy rolled her eyes. "If you say so. You two should learn to live a little."

At this point, Maisy's friend Guy returned with a waiter. Guy was holding two drinks and the waiter was holding two and a small plastic tray holding a bill and a pen.

"I thought this would save us some time trying to chase down drinks later," said Guy. "It's incredibly busy at all the bars."

The waiter, trying to juggle the two drinks and the bill, accidentally let go of one of the drinks. The glass hit the floor and most of its contents sprayed up on Maisy. Her face was purple with anger and her hands shook. She was livid. Maisy immediately launched into a tirade on the hapless waiter while Miles did his best to move as far away as possible to indicate he had nothing to do with the screaming harpy nearby. He opened his eyes wide to Myrtle and she nodded and said quietly to Guy, "Goodbye."

"Wow," said Myrtle, after they'd finally gotten out of earshot of the yelling Maisy. "She has some temper."

"Like mother, like daughter," said Miles. "I don't remember Celeste being particularly mild-mannered."

"Seeing that kind of outburst makes me wonder if Maisy might be our murderer. After all, Celeste's murder doesn't exactly seem to have been planned. To me, it's more likely that the killer knocked on Celeste's door and was obviously let in since the killer was close to Celeste. Whoever it was might have started arguing with her and then grabbed the nearest heavy object in a cloud of anger. In a panic, they'd have wanted to get rid of the body," said Myrtle. "And Maisy seems to fit that profile to a T. We've seen her angry—that poor waiter."

Myrtle and Miles sat down in a small conversation area close enough to hear the pianist in the lounge behind them. They spent a few, quiet moments listening to the classic music playing and looking at the beautiful landscape out the window.

Miles said, "Right. But don't you think that Celeste could have made *anyone* that mad? She seemed to have a gift for upsetting people. I bet Celeste could even infuriate the angelic Eugenia if she'd tried. And Maisy seemed to indicate that Terrell was positively seething with bitterness over his mother's influence in his life."

"Yes, she certainly did that," said Myrtle. "Which makes me wonder why she's so keen to implicate him. There doesn't seem to be any love lost between brother and sister. Besides, Maisy is one to talk about influence. From every indication, Celeste had Maisy completely under her control. Maisy even bought new and Celeste-unapproved clothing for the cruise. And she's taking the opportunity to live it up without her mother around."

Miles said, "True. But it's obvious that Maisy was on the point of rebelling anyway. She seemed to be enjoying rubbing her behavior in her mother's face. She didn't have to kill her to get her independence ... she was having her teenage rebellion thirty years late."

"I wish we'd had the chance to talk to Maisy a little longer," said Myrtle.

"Really? I'd relish the opportunity to never talk to Maisy again," said Miles fervently.

Myrtle said, "I wanted to know why she said that her mother was 'a horrid friend to Bettina.' Bettina certainly hasn't indicated that they had a rocky relationship in any way."

"That might just be Maisy being spiteful," said Miles. He yawned. "I know I'm supposed to take advantage of the nighttime entertainment, but I'm completely exhausted. I'm going to have to call it a night. The combination of glaciers and investigating is apparently very tiring. What are we doing tomorrow? I've forgotten."

"Well, I for one am going ashore. In fact, I offered to go ashore with Jack so that Red and Elaine could have some time together," said Myrtle. "They can shop or tour or eat a quiet meal or do whatever they want."

"So, if it's tomorrow," said Miles, staring at the ceiling as if the trip itinerary might be thoughtfully printed up there, "it must be ...."

"We have a choice between Haines and Skagway," said Myrtle. "Jack and I are going to Haines because it's allegedly quieter than Skagway. But it's still picturesque and I can take more pictures to accompany my fantastic article for the *Bugle*."

"Do you need any help with toddler corralling?" asked Miles. "It seems like trying to herd a toddler boy in an unfamiliar city would be difficult."

"Not at all. Jack is always the perfect angel when he's with me—I'm not sure what's wrong with Red and Elaine that he acts up with them. Anyway, I mainly want to find a place that has free Wi-Fi and check my messages on my phone. Maybe a café or something where Jack can snack and I can pull up a signal. I wrote an update for the *Bugle* and I want to send it and a couple of pictures along to Sloan. That way he can get a trip update now and then I can send the big story after we're home."

Miles said, "I thought you already sent Sloan an update."

"Yes, but that was just the Denali portion of the trip. I need to update everyone on the cruise—they've got to be waiting for information," said Myrtle impatiently.

"Why do I feel doubtful that that's the case?" asked Miles.

"Of course they are. Bradley residents are stuck in a cultural desert, Miles. They're being subjected in their newspaper to foolishness about Tristan Buroker's ham radio hobby. Believe me, the *Bugle* readers are eager for an armchair escape."

Miles wisely decided not to challenge this. "There's that library on the top deck. The Crow's Nest. They have Wi-Fi there."

"At an outrageous fee and for a very slow connection? No, thank you. No, I plan on finding Wi-Fi like a detective," said Myrtle.

"How is that?"

Myrtle said, "I'll follow a crew member. I bet they hop off the ship and immediately go right to wherever the free Wi-Fi is."

Miles hesitated. "I was planning on going on the bicycle ride. The glacier fjord one."

"When is that?"

Miles said, "It's supposed to be at nine in the morning."

"Oh, well, Jack and I certainly aren't going off the ship at nine. Half the shops probably don't open until later. He and I were going after lunch. Plenty of time for you to join us after your ride," said Myrtle.

"Do *you* want to go on the bike excursion with me?" asked Miles. "It's only seven miles and the course is supposed to be fairly flat. We're to see nesting eagles and spawning salmon and bears."

Myrtle gave him a surprised look and then laughed. "Thanks for the compliment. Although I'm in excellent mental and physical shape, there might be a rule out there about octogenarians and bicycles. No thanks; I'm going to keep my bones intact during the trip. I'll see you after lunch and you can join up with Jack and me."

Chapter Eight

The next morning, Myrtle was finishing up lunch with Jack at the ship's largest buffet restaurant. Jack had lots of chicken fingers and Myrtle had indulged in salmon once more. "Oh look," said Myrtle to Jack. "There's Mr. Miles."

Jack peered thoughtfully at Miles as he slowly approached, carrying a plate of food. "Him tired," he said knowledgeably.

"I believe you're right, Jack," said Myrtle with a smile. To Miles she said, "Jack says you look tired. Was it really only seven miles, or did your guide get lost and make it longer?"

"Sadly, it was only seven miles. But it wasn't all flat. Or maybe I'm just completely out of shape. I'm going to be sore tomorrow, no doubt," said Miles, grimacing. He sat down next to Jack. "The bald eagles were beautiful, though. And it was *so good* to be on dry land." He squinted across the room and suddenly looked alarmed. "Oh no. It's that Violet."

"What? Surely her dreadful book club isn't starting *today*," said Myrtle.

"It's not as if there are unlimited days on the ship," reminded Miles.

"Have we been spotted?" asked Myrtle.

"I'm afraid so," said Miles. He looked panicky. "I don't think I can handle any fun books today."

Violet was upon them immediately. She said with concern, "Did you forget? The book discussion? It was only earlier this morning that I mentioned it, but with people our age .... "

Myrtle said emphatically, "I'm spending time with my grandson today and I don't think any of you would like to hear fun truck books, which is what you'd get as Jack's contribution."

Miles added hastily, "Myrtle and I checked our schedules and between excursions and helping with Jack, our schedule is completely full."

Violet frowned. "Is it? That's so odd. Red was sure that Myrtle's schedule, in particular, was free of excursions."

"He must have forgotten how busy I was," said Myrtle. "But thanks anyway."

As Violet walked away, Miles started breathing again. "A narrow escape."

"I think Red needs reminding that he's not my social secretary," said Myrtle, eyes narrowed.

"You don't exactly have your gnome collection with you," said Miles.

"I'll have to figure something out." Myrtle's mind was already in overdrive.

Miles pulled the acupressure band off his wrist and handed it to Myrtle. "By the way, do you want this? I don't think Celeste needs it anymore. And, after being on land, I think I've reset myself. I now officially have regained my sea legs. I'd rather not bring up my whole seasickness problem by trying to return the band to one of Celeste's offspring."

Myrtle slid the band into her purse. "If you're sure. I guess you know where to find me if it flares up again. I'm keeping mine on, at any rate. Why mess with success?"

After eating, Myrtle, Miles, and Jack disembarked to walk into Haines. Miles said, "I know your plan was to follow the crew to find Wi-Fi, but surely they'd have gotten off earlier to check their email or whatever."

"Yes, but there are *many, many* crew members on this ship, Miles. They couldn't *all* hop off at the first opportunity—there must be shifts of some kind." She squinted in the bright sunshine and then said, "See? There goes several of the crew now. Let's follow them."

Miles sighed. "They're pretty far ahead of us, Myrtle."

"Well, we don't have to *catch up*. We can merely keep them in our sights. I believe they'll lead us to the Wi-Fi pot of gold. You can't tell me that they don't want to go online. And the ship's Wi-Fi is horrid."

They followed the men alongside the sea and down some side streets. Miles was moving slower than usual. "Are we *sure* they're going in search of Wi-Fi, Myrtle? Perhaps they're simply out to cash their paychecks at the bank."

"We can't catch up with them to ask. Just have faith, Miles." Although it was a bit more of a walk than Myrtle had reckoned on, it was still fairly short. She'd had in her mind that the crew would disembark and head right to the closest business.

Miles peered anxiously at Jack's short legs. "Are we sure Jack can make it? I'm not sure I can carry him all the way back."

"Oh, pooh. Jack has more energy than you and me and ten other people put together do," said Myrtle. "Just don't *you* run out of energy. I certainly can't carry *you* back." She squinted again. "Look! The men have dodged into that wooden structure there. The lovely one with the two-story picture window."

Miles said, "It's the Haines Borough Library, apparently."

Myrtle beamed at him. "Bingo! Wi-Fi, here we come."

The light, airy, and cheerful library had lovely views of the outdoors. Myrtle took a piece of paper with the Wi-Fi instructions from the front desk. Then she got Jack settled first with paper, pencils, and lots of picture books that she helped him pick out.

"Is he going to sit still?" asked Miles doubtfully. "He doesn't even seem fatigued by the walk."

"It was a short walk, Miles! Maybe it just doesn't seem that way for people who've biked seven miles. Jack loves reading. I'd say we're good for thirty minutes."

Miles had no desire to check his messages, preferring instead to peruse magazines. Myrtle carefully followed the Wi-Fi instructions and logged into her email account.

Sloan had written her: *Can't wait for you to come back, Miss Myrtle. I gave up transcribing Wanda's notes. I went ahead and decided she was valuable enough to the paper to get her a pay-as-you-go phone, which the Bradley Bugle is paying for. Now she's telling me the horoscopes over the phone and I'm translating them into the King's English for the paper. The only problem now is that her electricity has been turned off for non-payment so she can't charge the phone. I reckon the paper will be paying for her power bill, too.*

Myrtle responded to Sloan's email and carefully attached her first article for the *Bugle* along with what she fondly considered her professional-level pictures.

Myrtle checked the next message and made a face. Erma had also sent her an email. Usually, she sent Erma's emails directly into the trash, but since she *was* away from home and Erma *was* her next-door neighbor, Myrtle decided to make an exception this time.

Erma said: *I knew that you'd want to be left in the loop while you were out of town. The truth is that I've been suffering terrible, debilitating stomach pains ....*

Myrtle grimaced and skimmed until she got to a different section of Erma's too-long epistle.

I've had Dusty around to hang some pictures and replace a window screen for me. I asked him if he wanted to provide you with an update, and he did. I will say that your horrid beast Pasha has been set on a course to terrify your Puddin at every opportunity. Picture attached. I braved my horrific allergies to take this as proof.

Myrtle studied the attached photo. It showed Pasha, fur standing on end, fangs showing, ears back, facing off with Puddin, eyes open wide, snarling. Which looked more ferocious, Myrtle couldn't decide. "Poor, dear Pasha," she muttered to herself. "Being terrorized by the Wicked Puddin."

Dusty, surprisingly, appeared to write better than he spoke. Although he apparently had some sort of aversion to punctuation. His note read:

House fine and yard fine and cat fine and hot here

Miles glanced up from his perusal of *The Economist*. "Anything interesting?"

"No. Everything is fine and as usual. Pasha is keeping Puddin on her toes."

Miles nodded and continued reading.

Myrtle responded to the emails quickly and then said, "Okay, I guess we need to figure out where we should go from here. I bet the librarians have some ideas of where to take a toddler in Haines."

Miles said, "The library was the perfect activity, although I never would have guessed it. He's been completely absorbed. I bet we could stay here until the ship leaves."

Myrtle shook her head. "First rule of toddler caretaking, Miles: always quit an activity while you're ahead."

The friendly staff suggested that Myrtle and Miles take Jack to the American Bald Eagle Foundation. "They have stuffed animals there, but they also have live birds that are recuperating. Maybe you'll even be there when they feed them," suggested one of the librarians.

Fortunately for Miles, it wasn't too bad of a walk. Jack seemed to enjoy the museum, but the best part was when they came upon a recuperating bald eagle. "Bird!" he said ecstatically.

"It's tremendous," said Miles. "Somehow you don't realize how huge those birds are until you see them up close."

Myrtle nodded, distracted. Eugenia had just walked into the viewing area, wearing a tremendous, old, and clunky camera around her neck and an eager expression. She waved awkwardly when she spotted Myrtle, Miles, and Jack, and hurried over.

"Just look at this beautiful boy," she gasped, fumbling to take the lens cap off the camera. "Isn't he amazing?"

"He certainly is," said Miles fervently.

Eugenia said shyly, "I don't think I really even took the chance to thank you for helping me when I couldn't find Celeste. I felt so panicked and you were both so calm. Thanks for all your help. It almost seems like a bad dream now. Here I am, in front of this gorgeous bird, in this lovely place, and it's hard to believe that something so horrible happened to my poor aunt."

"Very true. Absolutely shocking what happened to Celeste," said Myrtle. "Although, the more of the family I've spoken to, the more a certain ... picture has emerged of your aunt. Sort of another side to her."

Eugenia automatically looked guilty. "I'm afraid we've all had our bad thoughts about poor Aunt Celeste from time to time. I feel just awful about it now. Imagine—all that bad energy that I was directing her way and then for something so dreadful to happen to her. And while she was kind enough to take us on this wonderful adventure in Alaska! It's terribly unfair to her."

Myrtle nodded sympathetically. "It must have been such a shock to you to discover that she was missing. How exactly did you learn that, by the way? Didn't you think that maybe she stepped out for a bite to eat or to watch a show?"

Eugenia shook her head decisively. "No, because Aunt Celeste always believed in routines and schedules. Even traveling, she tried to follow her routines. It kept her organized and clear-headed, she said. After dinner, I helped my aunt get ready for bed. Sometimes she had a hard time getting her arms out of sleeves and that sort of thing. Then I returned to my room for a while to relax. As usual, I returned to my aunt's room last night to give her some medications before she turned in—she was most insistent on receiving them at the same time each day. That's when I discovered that she wasn't *in* her cabin." Eugenia's eyes welled up with tears and she batted her eyelashes to try to discourage them.

Myrtle said, "And you immediately thought that something must have happened to her. Now I have an important question for you: who do you think was responsible for this?"

Eugenia put her hands up as if defending herself from the onslaught of questions. "I can't believe *anyone* I know would do something like this to Aunt Celeste. She was so kind to us! This trip!"

Jack was starting to get restless and Myrtle knew it was only a matter of time before she had to move on. She said a bit impatiently, "But surely, with all the time you've spent with your aunt, you've had the opportunity to observe things— conversations or arguments. You might be able to shed some insight here on who might have been irritated or upset with Celeste."

Miles handed Jack his pocket-sized camera in desperation since the three-year-old was gearing up for a potential breakdown. Myrtle gave a small groan. Didn't Miles remember what happened the last time he gave Jack an electronic device? Jack very ably reprogrammed it.

At least Myrtle appeared to have gotten through to Eugenia on some level. She was apparently thoughtfully considering various run-ins between her aunt and other family members. Finally, she said slowly, "This doesn't mean anything at all. It was only an observation of mine."

"Yes?" prompted Myrtle, trying her hardest to keep her patience as Jack now accidentally dropped Miles's camera on the floor and then scrabbled to pick it up, only to drop it again. Miles gave Myrtle a frantic look.

"Bettina. Oh, I hate saying this because Bettina has been very kind to me. A good friend. But Bettina did something very out of character on this trip. Rather spiteful. For some reason, she decided to play a prank on my aunt after bridge yesterday and pour ink from a black pen all over Aunt Celeste's nicest dress— the dress she planned on wearing to the formal night on the ship.

It was completely ruined. Aunt Celeste and I had to go to the shops on the ship to find something else for her to wear, which was *awful* because the shops were so expensive." Eugenia paused and her eyes welled up with tears. "Oh! Aunt Celeste never even had a chance to *wear* the dress!"

Now Myrtle was all brisk efficiency. She couldn't possibly handle a sobbing suspect and a tired toddler on her own. She tried to bring Eugenia back to critical thinking again, "And you've no idea why Bettina would do such a peculiar and malicious thing? From my own brief dealings with her, she simply doesn't seem like the catty type."

Eugenia, fortunately, got a grip on her emotions and said, "I've no idea. Maybe it was a reaction to something my aunt said or did. But I didn't overhear anything."

There was something in Eugenia's face, though, that made Myrtle think that she knew something. Eugenia was about as easy to read as a picture book. She couldn't look Myrtle in the eyes. Whether it was information about Bettina or something else, Myrtle couldn't say.

"Are you *sure* you didn't see or hear anything to do with your aunt's murder? Something even that you weren't sure what it meant at the time but are now thinking about it from a different angle?" asked Myrtle.

Again, Eugenia looked away and shook her head so that her hair fell into her face.

Thinking back to her conversation with Bettina, Myrtle said, "Speaking of overhearing things, were you aware of the new will that your aunt had written?"

Eugenia instantly flushed, which told Myrtle in no uncertain terms that she had been aware. She said miserably, "I did overhear that, although I didn't mean to. My aunt was always talking about her will. But this time she did sound as if she meant to change it or *had* changed it. Yes, I knew."

Jack gave Miles's camera one more drop for good measure and Myrtle said quickly to Eugenia, "Well, I'm sure it all seems like a mess, but we'll work through it. Sorry to distract you from your touring. I should go—my grandson ...."

Eugenia nodded, seeming relieved at being abruptly dismissed. "Of course. I should go, anyway. I've pulled my back somehow and I probably should go lie down or try to stretch."

"Maybe you should try the ship's hot tub," suggested Miles. "It's in the pool area. Maybe it could help to loosen up your muscles."

"Thanks—that's a great suggestion. I may have to try that after I stretch. I'll see you both around." Eugenia moved away.

Myrtle stooped down next to Jack. "Let's take a picture, you and me."

Miles said glumly, "If it even takes pictures anymore. It may now be a rather expensive paperweight."

"Nonsense! Besides, you definitely need to replace this old dinosaur of a camera, worst case scenario," said Myrtle with a sniff.

She gingerly took the camera from Jack, positioned it at the eagle, let Jack look through the viewfinder, and then showed Jack how to snap the photo.

Miles said under his breath, "So it still takes pictures. But can you remove it from his clutches without creating a scene?"

Myrtle gave Miles a supercilious look. "Jack, why don't we go to the gift shop and you can pick out something from your Nana."

"Pure genius," murmured Miles as Myrtle handed him back the camera.

"It's about time you recognized that," said Myrtle.

The gift shop had lots of different items in it. But the only thing that Jack had his eye on was a tremendous snow globe made of solid glass. It had a rather lovely Alaskan landscape in it and a bald eagle featured prominently.

"Bird!" said Jack excitedly. He pointed to the snow globe.

"Is that what you want from your Nana?" asked Myrtle. She peered at the price, squinted, and then said, "Well, you certainly have good taste."

Miles said doubtfully, "Myrtle, don't you think you should ... er ... redirect the young man in question? Something tells me that Red isn't going to be happy having to cart around a seven or eight-pound snow globe in his suitcase and fly it back home."

"Pooh. It's not seven or eight pounds." Myrtle, however, when she experimentally lifted the souvenir, discovered otherwise. "It'll be fine. I'll put it in my own luggage if I need to. Besides, it serves him right. Trying to set me up with a book club at sea. Ridiculous."

"When your bag goes over the limit and you have to pay a surcharge to the airline, you're not going to feel the same way," said Miles. "Why don't you show him these beautiful stuffed bald eagles?"

But Jack would not be dissuaded and Myrtle wasn't too interested in trying. "It's a lovely souvenir of a fun trip," she said as she took it to the cashier.

When they finally returned to the ship, however, Red immediately agreed with Miles. She'd dropped Jack off by Red and Elaine's stateroom and Red took one look at the snow globe and moved their conversation out into the narrow hall so Jack wouldn't overhear them. "Let's head back to your room. What on earth were you thinking, Mama? That thing weighs a ton."

"I'll take it in my bag," said Myrtle as they walked down the hall. "I'm sure I'm under the bag limit for the flight."

"Not just that, but what if he drops it on his foot or something? It would break a bone or two, for sure."

Myrtle, who had sort of envisioned Jack putting the snow globe on a shelf and gazing reverently at it from time to time at a safe distance, frowned. She certainly didn't want Jack to get hurt by it.

Red was clearly trying to be polite about the whole business. That was likely because Myrtle was doing a fair amount of babysitting for them. "I appreciate the idea and the fact that you were getting something that Jack wanted, but if you don't mind returning it?"

"Returning it? How would I do that? The ship has already set sail and we're on our way to Juneau. I can't exactly tell the crew to turn around so I can return a trinket." A rather expensive trinket.

"Juneau will be perfect. These gift shops all sell pretty much the same stuff and Juneau is *loaded* with shops. I'm sure there's someone there who will take it off your hands. Or one of the other ports, if you've got plans at Juneau," said Red.

"All right, all right. I'll keep it in my room in the meantime and Jack can visit it a little before I return it. I'll just explain to him that his father is mean," said Myrtle in exasperation. "And stay out of my business, by the way."

Red blinked, trying to look innocent.

"You know what I'm talking about," Myrtle growled. "The book club thing."

"Now, Mama. You know how you love books. I was just looking out for you."

"*Books*. I love *books*. Not whatever Violet is trying to pass off as books." Then Myrtle turned suddenly pleasant again as she realized that she needed something from Red. Information. "Anyway, how are things going with the case? Any leads?"

Red sighed and leaned against his cabin door. "Well, you know I'm really just working it part-time. The ship or the cruise line doesn't care if I solve the case or not. I've come to the conclusion that Celeste was likely the brightest person in her family, that's for sure." He spoke in a low voice and looked quickly in both directions down the hall to make sure the family wasn't lurking around.

"I'd have to agree with you there. Even Terrell's brain isn't all he thinks it is. And they're all just a little batty. Bettina seems nice. She'd most likely be a friend if she lived in Bradley," said Myrtle.

Red said, "No matter what they say, most of them likely knew that Celeste was talking about changing her will. That's because Celeste appeared to have had an unsavory habit of *telling* people she was considering excluding them from her will. Most of the time they knew that she was giving idle threats but I think there was something different this time and she was more serious."

"Threatening to cut family out of a will is a dangerous practice, to be sure," said Myrtle.

"Aside from that, I've got nothing yet. They all *could* have done it, easily, with that heavy champagne bottle. They all seem to have had a somewhat bumpy relationship with her. And they all could easily have popped into her room, killed her, and thrown her overboard," said Red. "The throwing overboard would have taken more effort, but Celeste wasn't all that big."

"And you're still the only one checking into her death at all?" asked Myrtle. "The ship hasn't even recognized that they've lost a passenger, from what I've seen."

"As I mentioned before, they want to keep it hush-hush. But they are having a small memorial service for Celeste in the ship's chapel tomorrow while we're docked in Juneau," said Red with a shrug. "They're certainly not going to want to advertise that there was a murder onboard so it would be referred to as a natural death, if anyone asks. And, before you ask, the security guy is still laid out with that vile stomach illness."

Myrtle made a face. "I may not update Miles on his condition. He's paranoid about catching germs as it is. He'll end up camping out at the hand sanitizing station for the rest of the cruise."

After Red left, Myrtle picked up the phone and called the front desk. She put on her best little old lady voice. "Yes. Have you got a concierge? You're one? Excellent. Have you got an internet connection and a printer? I need you to do me a tremendous favor."

Chapter Nine

Juneau was so rainy that Myrtle realized how lucky they'd been with the weather so far on the cruise. The rain was pouring down in buckets through the foggy air. There was a tram that lifted passengers past a dense Alaskan rainforest to the top of a mountain ... at least, that's what it was supposed to do. Myrtle couldn't even see the tram out her window for the rain and fog.

There was a tap at her cabin door and she opened it. Miles stood there looking rather bemused. "Your door. How ... ?"

"Oh, you mean the gnomes on my door? Aren't they the dearest things? Can you believe that there is a concierge on this ship? So very cooperative, too. She was delighted to print out a bunch of gnome pictures and bring me tape to put them up on the door," said Myrtle. She and Miles sat on her sofa together.

"The concierge must have thought you were insane," said Miles, shaking his head.

"Certainly not. I told her the pictures were for Jack. She couldn't be happier to help me out," said Myrtle.

"I'm wondering if I should make a bet with Elaine," said Miles thoughtfully. "We could bet on how long Red will allow those gnomes to be stuck on your stateroom door before he pulls them all off."

"At least my point will have been made," said Myrtle. "That's all that really matters. Now, what are we doing today?"

"I'd really planned on being on the tram. Now it's too foggy to see anything. I don't want to ride a tram with no view." He sounded quite dispirited.

"I thought you were Mr. Adventure," said Myrtle. "Isn't there some sort of zipline thing or something?"

Miles gave her a long-suffering look. "I don't want to *dangle* over the rainforest; I simply want to view it. And it appears we're completely socked in with rain."

"Then let's go shopping. I want to get some smoked salmon to bring home with me as a souvenir of the trip. And Red is forcing me to try to pawn off the snow globe on some poor shopkeeper as a return."

Miles said, "But you wouldn't have purchased it at their store."

"Red says all the stores sell the same stuff and that it shouldn't be hard to get them to accept it." Myrtle shrugged.

"Maybe. But not to pay *you* back for it!" said Miles.

"At any rate, I'm supposed to try. Believe me, I agree with you—it's ridiculous. It's one reason why there are gnomes taped all over my door. The snow globe cost too much for me to write it off as a loss. And I need to find something else to give Jack," said Myrtle.

"Shopping it is, then," said Miles with a sigh. "Let's dig out our rain gear."

It was raining so hard when they left the ship that they found themselves rushing from one store to another and from one awning-covered bit of sidewalk to another. What's more, no one was willing to take Jack's snow globe back.

"Bah," said Myrtle, shoving the souvenir into her massive pocketbook after her latest failed attempt at returning it. "I give up. I'll just keep it myself. Let's find Jack a stuffed animal and pick up some smoked salmon. Here's a shop we haven't been in yet."

They walked in and navigated around the huge tee-shirt display to find the stuffed animals and other goods. The shop was crowded with tourists from the ships.

Miles said under his breath, "Don't look now, but Maisy has just entered the shop."

Maisy had indeed walked in. She appeared to be perusing the magnet section of the shop. Myrtle said under her breath, "Let's talk to her. It will be good to hear from her when she's completely sober."

Maisy's mood was much improved by the lack of alcohol in her system. She greeted Myrtle and Miles cheerfully. She wore a nylon rain jacket and the hood covered her too-blonde hair. "Hi there! Killing a rainy day, like I am? I desperately needed to get off that ship. I didn't disembark when we were in Haines and Skagway, which was a huge mistake."

"It's good to be on dry land," agreed Myrtle. "And how are you doing, dear?" Myrtle fell easily into chatty old lady mode, once she realized that Maisy might be receptive to it today.

"Oh, it's all right. I'm on an Alaskan cruise, so things couldn't be *too* bad, you know? I guess you've heard that we're having a hastily-put-together memorial for Mother today?" Maisy gave them a questioning look. "None of us were too keen on the idea of having a big 'do' for her when we got home. We figured it was best to do it at sea and explain to everyone when we got home that we needed immediate closure."

Myrtle had the feeling that Celeste would have preferred the 'big do' at home, but she certainly wasn't around to lend her vote to the matter. She said, "I think it's a good idea. And Miles and I will come, of course."

"Of course," repeated Miles courteously, although he shot Myrtle a long-suffering look. He was no fan of funerals and he'd been to several of them recently in the days leading up to the trip.

Maisy said wryly, "That's very kind of you. I think I'd get out of it myself if I could. The family is fractious right now. Maybe it's just being trapped on the ship and that feeling that we can't escape each other. But Terrell, Randolph, and I are totally getting on each other's nerves. And meek Eugenia and loud Bettina are simply annoying. We'll all likely try very hard to stay out of each other's way once the service is over."

Myrtle affected a concerned expression. "What are Terrell and Randolph doing to be upsetting?"

"They're just so coarse!" said Maisy, waving a hand in the air.

Myrtle thought this was rather ironic, coming from Maisy.

"Terrell has been gloomily muttering how Eugenia shouldn't get a penny. He's complaining about Mother's rewrite of her will and saying darkly how he'll have his lawyers all over the document when we get back home. You know—he's just not happy about the money thing. And Randolph switches from egging Terrell on about the lawyers and the will, to being disgustingly gleeful about Mother's death. Randolph was definitely unhappy about the terms of the will and very unhappy with Eugenia."

Again, Myrtle found it ironic that Maisy would criticize anyone for being happy about her mother's death. Maisy seemed to be the happiest and most relieved of any of them when she'd gotten the news. But Myrtle gave her a sympathetic nod, anyway.

Maisy suddenly seemed bored with the conversation. She moved a few yards away from the magnets and into the tee shirts. "Which one do you like better?" she asked, pointing at two shirts.

Shopping with Maisy was mercifully short. Miles was at the end of his rope with both shopping and with Maisy, so they broke things off early and decided to catch a bite to eat in town as a change of pace. It was a wooden restaurant very close to where the ships were moored that offered the largest crab legs Myrtle and Miles had ever seen, served with hushpuppies. Myrtle had an appetizer of soup before knowing how big the crab legs were. She wondered if she'd ever eat again as she and Miles stumbled away in a food coma.

They boarded the ship in plenty of time to change into something less casual for Celeste's service. Miles tapped on Myrtle's door about fifteen minutes before it started.

The chapel was small and very cold. Randolph appeared to already have imbibed before the service. "I suppose it's five o'clock somewhere," murmured Miles disapprovingly. Terrell kept glancing at his watch. Maisy was dressed rather severely in what Myrtle imagined was an outfit her mother would have approved of. She was with her ponytailed friend Guy, who had inexplicably decided to wear a Hawaiian shirt and cut-off shorts. Bettina, on the other hand, was likely *over*dressed in a sparkly black dress with high heels and lots of flashy jewelry.

"Where's Eugenia?" asked Myrtle, glancing around the small room.

Miles said glumly, "Maybe she caught whatever the security guy has." His hands started moving, almost of their own volition, rubbing together as if they had imaginary hand sanitizer on them.

The service was extremely short.

Miles muttered, "Why can't we have more services like this one at home?" They stood at the close with the lone pianist giving a recessional.

"We can't, because ordinarily, the minister at home has actually *met* the deceased," said Myrtle. "Although this chaplain did give an extraordinary good general service under the circumstances. He somehow had the ability to make it feel personal." She peered at the family. "What are they doing? Do they not know what to do?"

The family apparently didn't. Maisy was uncertainly moving toward the chaplain, presumably to thank him on behalf of the family. Randolph appeared to have dozed off and was leaning heavily on the side of the pew. Terrell was walking with great determination toward the exit.

"For heaven's sake," hissed Myrtle. "These people. Have they never been to a funeral before? They're supposed to give us the opportunity to shake their hands or hug them and tell them how sorry we are."

Miles said, "Well then, why don't you catch Terrell and set him straight before he's back in the ship library doing crosswords?"

Myrtle and Miles quickly followed Terrell, Myrtle giving genteel coughs until she finally gave up with any pretext of subtlety and reached out her cane to jab him in the back of a leg as he left the chapel.

When Terrell whirled around, Myrtle said pleasantly, "We hoped the family was going to let us have the chance to say how sorry we are."

There was a flash of anger in his eyes. Whether Myrtle was solely responsible for it or whether it had to do with his feelings for his mother, she didn't know. He said coldly, "I assumed it; you didn't have to tell me."

Myrtle nodded. "All right. I did have one question for you. Where's Eugenia?"

"How do I know?" said Terrell furiously. "Am I her keeper?"

Miles said in a mild tone, "Have you seen her today at all?"

"No. But I haven't gone looking for her, either."

By this point, Maisy, Bettina, Randolph, and Guy were exiting the chapel.

"What's going on?" asked Maisy, raising her eyebrows at Terrell's flushed features.

"And where's Eugenia?" asked Bettina. "It's really odd that she's not here."

Myrtle noticed that Randolph looked away.

"Nothing's going on," spat Terrell. "This woman is looking for Eugenia, that's all. Nothing to do with me. Why should I care where that money-grubbing person is?"

At that moment, a solemn Red and a uniformed crew member walked around a corner to join them. He said, "I'm glad you're all still together for the service. What I've got to say may come as a bit of a shock."

He paused as if waiting for anyone to say they wanted to sit down. Everyone simply stared blankly at Red.

He continued on, quietly. "Eugenia was found dead in one of the ship's hot tubs this morning. I'm very sorry."

Chapter Ten

Red may have been expressing condolences, but his gaze was sliding thoughtfully from one face to another, searching for a reaction.

Myrtle was searching, too. What she noticed was that no one had much of a reaction at all to this news. It was almost as if they'd just been notified that the kitchen was out of salmon and they'd have to change their order at a restaurant.

The only one of the group who seemed to have any sort of a reaction at all was Bettina. She shook her head and said, "That poor child."

Terrell said petulantly, "Well, and *now* what happens to all that money and property? Surely Eugenia doesn't have a will. How stupid this all is."

Bettina's voice was sharp in response. "Respect for the dead, Terrell."

Maisy asked politely, as if she were a child who had just remembered her manners, "What happened to Eugenia? Did she ... well, was there some sort of medical event?"

"Did she drown?" asked Randolph, frowning. "Too much to drink and then fell asleep?"

Terrell snorted. "That little mouse, drink? I never saw her drink."

"So now she's a mouse?" asked Maisy with a hard note in her voice. "You've been saying for the last couple of days that she was a schemer."

Red said carefully, "You're right. She didn't appear to have been drinking. She appeared to have been strangled."

The faces were all still blank, although Bettina put her well-manicured hands in front of her mouth.

"What on earth was she doing in a hot tub anyway?" blustered Terrell. "That hardly seems the kind of place she would go."

"Perhaps she was trying to pick someone up," said Randolph with a slight smile on his lips. "After all, she'd just become an heiress."

Miles cleared his throat. "Actually, Myrtle and I can likely offer some insight on that. We spent some time with Eugenia in Haines. She had either pulled a muscle or overworked one somehow. We recommended that she might want to use the hot tub as therapy for it."

"How sad that someone took advantage of that opportunity," said Myrtle, giving them all a hard look.

Red said, "You're all free to be on your way, but I'll be wanting to talk to each of you in the next couple of days."

Maisy said in an angry tone, "It's unbelievable that the ship isn't doing anything about this."

"I agree, but that's just not the way it works on the sea," said Red smoothly. "The security man they have is out of commission and wouldn't be launching much of an investigation even if he weren't."

The family dispersed, muttering to themselves as Myrtle, Miles, and Red looked thoughtfully after them. Red said, "Mama, you need to really watch your step. You made it sound as if you and Eugenia have been hanging out. If someone killed Eugenia because of what she knew, they might well think that you know the same information she did."

Myrtle said huffily, "Maybe Eugenia wasn't killed because of what she knew. Maybe she was killed because it looked as if she were going to inherit all of Celeste's money."

"If that was the reason someone murdered her, it was a completely ignorant decision. The money would go into probate and much of it would be used up by the courts. And who knows—maybe Eugenia was forward-thinking enough to create her own will. No, I suspect that it had more to do with Eugenia's proximity to her aunt. She would have been best positioned to see someone going into or out of her aunt's stateroom."

"I wonder when it happened?" said Myrtle. "I really feel sorry for the girl. She had a chance at a little freedom and it was immediately taken from her."

"I don't know. That's the problem with being on a ship and not having a forensic team to call on. And the hot tub obviously interfered with her body temperature so even if she had been dead for a while, I wouldn't have been able to tell. But common sense tells me that she couldn't have been there too long before she was discovered. There are too many people on the ship and the hot tubs are popular." Red looked at Miles. "Miles, can you make sure my mother spends the rest of the day in a complete waste of her time? Maybe watching a movie or her soap opera or playing bridge?"

Miles said, "I'll do my best."

Red said, "And Mama, I saw those blasted gnomes. I know you're not happy with me. I'm just trying to keep you safe, that's all."

Myrtle bared her teeth in a smile. "Red, you have nothing to worry about. I've no desire to court danger, believe me."

But it was clear, looking into Red's skeptical eyes, that he didn't.

As a matter of fact, Miles and Myrtle *did* spend the rest of the day quietly. But that was mainly due to the fact that Celeste's family had decided to spend their day in their rooms instead of out on the ship. Myrtle and Miles went to the ship library and read for a while with the beautiful scenery as a backdrop through the windows.

But the next morning, Myrtle was ready to talk to some suspects. *Early* the next morning. Since she'd had such a quiet day and had turned in so early the night before, she was wide awake at four a.m. Myrtle lay in bed for a little while to see if she could fall back asleep before giving up completely. She got up, showered, dressed, worked on the *Bradley Bugle* article, and decided to walk around the ship. Maybe Miles hadn't been able to sleep either and she'd see him wandering, too. The only problem with the ship was that she couldn't walk by his room to see if his lights were on the way she could at home.

Myrtle walked down a long hallway of wall-to-wall red carpet with chairs scattered to the sides. One of those chairs had a male figure in them and as she got closer, she saw that it was Randolph. As a bonus, he even appeared to be sober. He glanced up as she approached and gave her a small wave. She sat down across from him.

"You're up very early," she said. "I didn't expect to see anyone yet."

Randolph gave her a small smile. "I'm not up very early, I'm turning in very late. I haven't gone to bed yet."

And indeed, on closer inspection, Myrtle noticed the dark circles under his eyes and the fact that his clothes were a lot more wrinkled than they would be for someone who'd just gotten dressed. Although he still appeared as handsome as ever. It was unfair how well some men aged, thought Myrtle for the hundredth time.

Myrtle said, "Is that normal for you, or was it just the upsetting events from yesterday?"

"Both. It can certainly be normal, but it was a lot more likely that I would have been feeling really anxious after what happened to Eugenia," said Randolph. He sighed and looked morosely out the window next to him. "This constant daylight probably isn't helping things, either."

"I don't know," said Myrtle lightly, "I rather like having daylight when I'm up at odd hours. It makes me feel as though I'm not the only person on the planet who isn't sleeping." They both looked out the window at a bear they could see loping around the shore. Myrtle decided to warm Randolph up a bit with some easy questions. "You and Celeste seemed very different to me. How did the two of you meet?"

"Did we seem different?" asked Randolph. "I suppose we were. I think we both liked having fun. That may have been the main thing that we had in common. Celeste and I met in Las Vegas. I was gambling at the tables there and we hit it off. Actually, we hit it off enough for us to marry there."

"Really?" asked Myrtle, astounded. "I thought that Celeste didn't seem the type to head off to Las Vegas. Didn't she want Maisy to dress modestly and all that?"

"Oh, that's just because she'd convinced Maisy that she wasn't attractive enough to play up her assets," said Randolph. "As for Celeste heading off to Vegas? I don't think that was something she ordinarily did, no. But that momentary impulse was fate, I suppose."

Myrtle nodded. Her voice grew more serious as she said, "I'm worried, Randolph. Whoever is behind these murders is very dangerous. They've killed twice and gotten away with it—what's to stop them from killing again? I mean to find out who's behind these deaths."

Randolph turned to face her again, a bit of grudging respect in his eyes. "All right. I suppose you have questions for me then, is that it? I've already spoken to your son. He also seems quite determined to figure this out."

Myrtle nodded. "He probably told you that he doesn't have a very clear idea when Eugenia might have died. When did you last see her? Miles and I actually saw her in Haines for a bit at a bald eagle exhibit, but I haven't seen her since then." She gave Randolph a hard look, remembering how he'd glanced away at the mention of Eugenia earlier.

Randolph cleared his throat. "I'm afraid I'm not very good at keeping track of all the various people in our party."

Myrtle said, "No? I could have sworn that you knew something about Eugenia before Red broke the news of her death."

"How imaginative you are," said Randolph coolly. "And what a delightful trait for one of our seniors."

This annoyed Myrtle since she considered Randolph a senior, himself. Maybe not nearly *as* senior as Myrtle, but certainly a recipient of a discount whenever he went shopping. She said sharply, "And how evasive *you* are. Back to the original question: when was the last time you saw Eugenia?"

Randolph sighed and looked away. "Unfortunately, it all runs together. The drinking, you know. I really should stop. But it's so much harder to stop than you'd think, and it never seems to be a good time. There always seems to be some sort of stressful event going on. Like this interview."

"So you don't remember the last time you saw Eugenia. Can you at least offer an opinion on who might have wanted to kill her?" asked Myrtle.

Randolph, still looking out the window, said, "Oh look! A whale. Extraordinary creatures." He paused to watch it for a moment and Myrtle allowed the silence to grow uncomfortable until Randolph said, "Honestly, it's hard for me to imagine who would want to kill that little Pollyanna. Eugenia was always such a cheerful helper for Celeste. Maybe we all despised her happy disposition and optimism since none of the rest of us shared it. I'd say the person most likely to have killed her was Maisy. I believe it rankled Maisy the most that Eugenia was such an indispensable help to her mother."

Myrtle raised her eyebrows. "That's interesting. I'd gotten the impression that your wife wasn't particularly happy with Eugenia's care."

Randolph shrugged. "Celeste didn't suffer fools lightly. And Eugenia sometimes needed more instructions than Celeste thought was necessary. But did Celeste think that Eugenia was altogether more capable than her daughter? Most definitely."

"All right. But surely you're not suggesting that Maisy killed Eugenia because she was *jealous* of her?" said Myrtle.

"Why not? Although you're probably right—it would be more than just jealousy. It might also be the fact that Eugenia was inheriting all the money that we thought was going to *us*."

Myrtle said, "It's funny. Maisy suggested that *you* weren't particularly amused about the terms of Celeste's will. By the way, did you know that I found it? I'm good at that kind of thing."

"An unusual talent, to be sure. Amused by the will? No, I was highly annoyed by the will. It was just Celeste engaging in silly games, as usual, playing us all off of each other. I've no doubt that she changed her will in a fit of pique with every intention to change it back again once we started behaving ourselves. So, yes, the fact that Celeste died without having the chance to tear up the document was upsetting to me. I don't think that Eugenia deserved all of Celeste's estate and I've complained about it in Maisy's presence. But if I spoke out against Eugenia, Maisy was the hallelujah chorus. Believe me, she was unhappy with the arrangement, too."

Myrtle nodded. "Did you see Maisy or any of the family early yesterday morning or that night before?"

Randolph looked wearily at her. "What part of 'it all runs together' do you not understand? I've seen all of them out and about but I couldn't tell you when for the life of me." He stood up, with a great deal of effort. "And now, if you'll excuse me, I think it's time for me to turn in. I wouldn't want to miss ... where are we again today?"

Myrtle said, "Today is Ketchikan."

"Right. I wouldn't want to miss seeing Ketchikan." Although Randolph didn't sound so sure of that.

After talking with Randolph, Myrtle took a stroll around the ship. After that, she took her book out of her pocketbook to read until one of the restaurants opened for breakfast.

Miles joined her, looking like he badly needed the coffee in front of him.

"What happened to you?" asked Myrtle.

Miles said, "I just couldn't sleep. What a night."

"You should have gotten up. I was up very early having a conversation with Randolph," said Myrtle. She proceeded to fill him in.

Miles said, "So he thinks Maisy is responsible. I don't know. I'm not sure I can see her killing Eugenia. Maybe her mother, though. Honestly, the person with the strongest motive for Celeste's death was Eugenia. But I suppose she didn't do it."

"Unlikely. Although her motive is certainly strong," said Myrtle. She glanced at her watch. "What are your Ketchikan plans? I've forgotten."

"I'm to go salmon fishing," said Miles. "With any luck, I'll catch something."

"How is *that* supposed to work?" asked Myrtle. "Are you supposed to consume the thing right then and there on the boat? I can't see you lugging uncooked fish back in your suitcase or anything."

"No, they ship it home for me," said Miles. "For a fee."

"Sounds expensive."

Miles said, "What are *you* supposed to be doing in Ketchikan?"

"Taking in the fishing village and wildlife from a trolley bus. Totem poles, eagles, water features and whatnot. I didn't feel like walking it and I understand the sidewalks get crowded," said Myrtle. "Besides, I've already had a walk around the ship today. That's what happens when I've got insomnia—lots of exercise."

Miles was about to take another long sip of coffee, but abruptly set the coffee cup down and gave a fake smile to someone above Myrtle's shoulder. Myrtle turned and saw Bettina bearing a plate filled with eggs, bacon, sausage, and pancakes.

Bettina gave Myrtle a wink. "Nothing like being on vacation. The calories don't count on vacation, didn't you know? What are you two doing today?"

"Hi, Bettina," said Myrtle. "Want to sit with us?"

"I would, but I told Maisy I'd sit with her," said Bettina.

"To answer your question, I'm salmon fishing," said Miles.

Myrtle said, "And I'm on one of those trolley tours."

Bettina lifted her eyebrows. "Trolley tour? I'll be on that one with you. Great! I wasn't fancying sitting through a tour by myself. See you then. Ta-ta!" And she made her way off to find Maisy.

Miles said, "Why do I sense a grilling session ahead?"

"Oh, it won't be that bad for Bettina. I can ask her tons of questions in a purely conversational way. After all, it's completely natural that I'd be nosy—how often do murders happen?"

Miles said dryly, "I'd say they happen altogether too much."

"At any rate, I'll be very measured in my questioning. Bettina seems friendly. What's most important is, that she probably has lots of insights on these people since she's spent so much time around the family. Her perspective will be useful," said Myrtle.

"Nana!" called a little voice.

Myrtle reached out her arms and gave Jack a huge hug. "Jack! Have you had fun today?" She looked at a tired Elaine. "It looks like you've already had a long today and it's only breakfast."

Elaine nodded and carefully put their plates down on the table and sat down with Myrtle and Miles. "He was up early, so we walked around a little bit."

"I'm surprised I didn't see you," said Myrtle. "I did the same thing."

Red walked up in time to overhear them. "On a ship this big, it's pretty easy to avoid running into each other. Ask any of my suspects," he said in a wry voice.

Although Myrtle would have loved to press Red on this point, the conversation seemed to be going in more cruise-oriented patterns, courtesy of an always-polite Miles. "What are your plans for the day?" he asked Elaine.

Red, out of sight of Elaine, rolled his eyes at Miles and his mother.

Elaine said, "Oh, I'm so excited about today. You know those little flyers they put by our doors with the day's activities? There were some good ones on there. Red will hang out with Jack during his naptime and I'm going to the enrichment event onboard."

"You're not going into Ketchikan?" asked Myrtle.

"Only briefly—right after breakfast," said Elaine. "And then, after that, I'm going to make pottery."

Red looked pained. He'd had a lot of experience with Elaine's hobbies over the years. None of them ever turned out particularly well. Elaine had an adventurous spirit and longed for the creative life. Her talent, unfortunately, didn't accompany her longing.

Myrtle said, "Pottery? But surely there can't be a kiln onboard?"

"But there actually *is*," said Elaine excitedly. "According to the activity sheet, it's a 'seagoing kiln.' So we can 'throw pots', which is what the pros call it when you make them, then they fire them and we paint them. The class is in two parts—the making of the pot and the decorating of it later."

Elaine stopped chatting to help Jack cut up some fruit on his plate into a size that he could eat. Myrtle leaned over to Red. "You know what I think?"

"What?" murmured Red. "That this sounds nearly as disastrous as her knitting or her cross-stitch? Or her ill-fated attempt at being a ham radio operator?"

"Those pots sound awfully *heavy*. Like Jack's snow globe. But I don't hear you nixing the pottery class," said Myrtle.

Red said, "As if I could. You know how Elaine is when she sets her mind on something. At least I'm not having to lug home her pots *and* Jack's souvenir." He paused. "You did get rid of the thing, didn't you?"

"Of course," said Myrtle coolly, crossing her fingers under the table. Maybe the storekeepers in Ketchikan would be more open to the idea. She'd give it a go once she got off that trolley.

Chapter Eleven

The trolley tour was actually more entertaining than Myrtle thought it might be. The fishing village of Ketchikan was very picturesque, and the driver took them out into an equally scenic landscape away from town where eagles flew and waterfalls fell. Myrtle took a great number of pictures.

Not only was the tour entertaining, but Bettina was, too. She could tell a good joke and a good story. Nothing was said about the last few days on the ship as they took in the sights of Ketchikan.

At least, nothing was said until Myrtle brought it up.

"This is really a lovely tour," said Myrtle. "But then, I even enjoyed Juneau and it poured that day. What did you do when we were in Juneau?"

Myrtle thought Bettina's expression closed up just a bit. Juneau was, after all, the port where Eugenia met her fate. At some point, anyway.

Bettina said, "Well, with the rain and everything, I decided to stay on the ship. I'd wanted to do the tram ride thing, but I certainly wasn't going to get on it and not even have a view of Juneau by the end. I stayed in my room and caught up on my sleep."

"What did you think of Eugenia? Was she a nice girl?" asked Myrtle.

Bettina said, "Well, what was *your* impression of her?"

She seemed genuinely curious, so Myrtle took a few seconds to think it through. "I thought she was nice," said Myrtle. "That's sort of a weak word, but I think it fit her well. She seemed to try hard, and to be responsible. She didn't, maybe, seem like the greatest intellectual, but she was pleasant to be around."

Bettina nodded. "You don't think of her as someone who was deliberately scheming to have Celeste give her a fortune?"

"If she was, she was a much better actress than I'd have ever guessed," said Myrtle.

Bettina said, "I totally agree. I don't think she had the intellect to be able to sustain a show like that for years. Besides, *no one* could make Celeste do anything she didn't want to do. If she didn't want to give her money to Eugenia, there was no one on the planet who could make it happen."

Myrtle said slowly, "I also think Eugenia was observant."

Bettina narrowed her eyes. "You're saying that she saw something that may have gotten her killed?"

"It's an idea." Myrtle paused. "One thing Eugenia told me, somewhat under duress, is that you had played a prank on Celeste."

To Myrtle's surprise, Bettina flushed a mottled shade of red. "I'm afraid I did. It might not have been my most mature moment."

Myrtle said, "What Eugenia *didn't* tell me is why you'd done such a thing. She didn't even manage a wild guess. And playing childish pranks doesn't exactly fit into my view of you."

Bettina sighed. "No. No, it's not really something I'd ordinarily do. But Celeste was fond of playing games as I've mentioned before. She was really something of a student of human nature. She'd get bored and set up various conflicts or situations as almost a lab experiment to see how people would react."

"What kind of an experiment did she set up for you?" asked Myrtle.

Bettina pressed her lips together tightly for a few moments as she relived the experience. "I spotted a letter in Celeste's stateroom. When she saw me looking at it, Celeste told me, oh so casually, that she had been seeing the man I've been dating at home. Dazzling him with her money and telling him all sorts of stories about me."

Myrtle raised her eyebrows. "Why on earth would she do that? She's married."

"She always wanted to be the center of everyone's attention. Maybe she was jealous of the relationship that Jim and I were developing. Maybe she just didn't like seeing someone in a happier relationship than the one she had with Randolph. Whatever the reason, she decided to reach out to him. Apparently, they went to plays and movies and things together." The words seemed distasteful to Bettina and she winced after they came out of her mouth.

"That must have made you very upset with Celeste," said Myrtle.

"It did," said Bettina wryly, "But I didn't kill her. Instead, I did something far cattier. I ruined her evening dress that she was planning on wearing to the dressy night on the ship. Ink all over it. She didn't raise a hand to stop me, either. After I took my anger out on her dress, it was all over and done with. I don't harbor bad feelings. Life's too short." She stared pointedly out the window as if she would rather be talking about the landscape visible through the window of the trolley.

But Myrtle wasn't quite ready to let that happen yet. "Who do you think might have killed Eugenia? Did you hear or see anything unusual?"

"All I know is gut instinct. I don't have any real clues or proof at all. But I think Randolph has been acting particularly unstable. The drinking is out of control—much worse than it was at home. And he seems like he's up all hours of the night. It sure would have been easy for him to notice Eugenia out on her own and kill her."

Bettina seemed tired of the conversation and interrupted Myrtle before she could respond positively or negatively to the idea of Randolph as the villain. "What's your friend doing today? Why isn't he on the trolley with you?"

"Oh, Miles wanted to do some salmon fishing. He thinks he's going to catch a bunch of fish and then ship them back home," said Myrtle.

"He's probably spending the day with Terrell then. I think Terrell had a salmon fishing excursion today. They probably both fancy themselves Hemingway, and the sad truth is that they may not get any bites at all." Bettina gave a short laugh and then her eyes narrowed thoughtfully as she considered Myrtle. "How long have you and Miles been a couple then?"

"A couple of what? Friends? Oh, it's been a while now," Myrtle shrugged.

"No, I mean a *couple*. In a relationship. You must have had a lot in common with Celeste for you both to have such young consorts." Bettina smirked.

"What? For heaven's sake. Miles and I are simply good friends. We have adventures together, do book club, watch TV. Friends." Myrtle put a slight stress on *friends*.

"He's retired, isn't he? What was his former occupation?"

Myrtle said, "Oh, he was an architect or some such."

"He's rather well-off then?" Bettina asked.

"I'd say he's comfortable," said Myrtle. She was now feeling quite annoyed.

Now Bettina had a cunning look in her eye. "So you're saying he's *available*. Good to know. He's a nice-looking man, you know."

Myrtle sniffed. "Perhaps. If one likes the quiet, intellectual type." Her tone implied that Bettina was neither quiet nor intellectual and should perhaps consider pursuing other options for her shipboard romance. If Bettina were going to be hanging out with Myrtle and Miles and trying to snare him all the time, it was going to become very, very tiresome.

After the trolley ride, Myrtle boarded the ship and walked back to her stateroom. She had a lot to think about and she wanted to spend a little bit of time alone to do it. As she was heading to her small sofa, she noticed Jack's snow globe on the desk and made a face. She'd forgotten to take it into Ketchikan with her to try one last time to make a return at one of the shops. And at this point, she had no intention of going back into the town. She'd just stuff the thing in her suitcase later and surely it would make the trip home just fine.

Myrtle found, after sitting on her sofa for a while and considering the deaths of two people and the remaining suspects, that she would rather just watch her soap opera for a while. Life always seemed better when compared with catastrophic tragedies endured by the characters on *Tomorrow's Promise*.

Almost as if by design, there was a knock on her door right when the opening credits of the soap were running. It was Miles, appearing freshly showered and not at all fishy, holding two iced teas.

They watched the show together and found themselves laughing a lot more than they usually did. But the plot on the soap was especially wacky and it was especially hard to take the peculiar switched-at-birth story seriously.

When the show had finished, Myrtle felt a lot cheerier than she had been. Even Miles was cheerier, and he'd come in already in a good mood.

"How was the fishing?" asked Myrtle.

"I caught a few," said Miles. "And I ended up spending the day with Terrell in the process."

"Poor you," said Myrtle.

"It wasn't so bad," said Miles. "Perhaps you misjudged him."

"Or perhaps he's simply cheerier now that his mother isn't around to badger him anymore," said Myrtle. "And pooh. I'd wanted the chance to talk to him about Eugenia's death."

"You can do that in an hour with me, if you want to. He and I are going to have a drink together and talk fishing. You're welcome to come along. In fact, I had a feeling that you'd *insist* on coming along," said Miles.

"I'm guessing this means that you didn't question him at all on Eugenia's unfortunate demise," said Myrtle.

"You guess correctly. My questioning went more along the lines of inquiries related to his usual fishing holes and his favorite lures," said Miles.

Myrtle said, "Speaking of questioning, I did talk to Bettina on the trolley."

"I had a feeling that might be the case. How did that go? It couldn't have been too bad. I can think of other members of that group that would be a lot worse to take a trolley ride with. Bettina seems all right." Miles reached for his iced tea and took a big sip.

Myrtle said, "Bettina will be pleased to hear that. Part of our conversation involved her plans to ensnare you in her web."

Miles choked on his tea and Myrtle pounded him unsympathetically on the back.

Miles finally managed in a gasping voice, "Myrtle, you must deliver me from Bettina."

"It's a big ship. I'm sure you can manage to avoid her. Your compliment wasn't exactly a ringing endorsement of her so I'm assuming you won't be missing out on a meaningful romance," said Myrtle.

Miles made a face. Then he said thoughtfully, "Speaking of avoiding her, that reminds me that Terrell said something similar."

Myrtle raised her eyebrows. "*Terrell* is trying to avoid her? She must be a panther."

Miles considered this for a moment. "I believe you must mean *cougar*. And no, I didn't mean that Terrell was avoiding *Bettina*. *He* was avoiding Eugenia."

"What? Eugenia?"

Miles said, "Yes. He seemed to think that she might have had some kind of a crush on him."

"On *Terrell*? I suppose there's no accounting for taste. He has the personality of that wall over there," said Myrtle. "At least I'll have something else to ask him about. Glad you mentioned it. I know you didn't ask about the murder, but just in general, what kind of opinion do you have of him?"

Miles said, "Well, his fishing stories were fairly unbelievable. But then, they're fish stories. That's sort of to be expected for the genre."

"Hmm. That makes sense for fishing, but I don't think that's the only point where he might embellish his abilities. There was his poor crossword puzzle performance to consider."

Miles nodded solemnly. He took crosswords nearly as seriously as Myrtle. "You think he might be lying about other things?"

"Once a liar, always a liar," said Myrtle. "I saw plenty of that when I was teaching school. With some kids you couldn't believe a word they said."

An hour later at the bar near the ship library, they saw Terrell sitting at a table with a full cocktail in front of him as he worked on a crossword.

"At least he doesn't drink like Randolph," murmured Myrtle.

Terrell stood up when they approached, but he didn't look any too pleased to see Myrtle there.

"You don't mind if my friend, Myrtle, joins us, do you?" asked Miles in a mild voice.

Terrell clearly *did* mind but wasn't about to say anything. He gave a stiff nod and then gestured to them as a waiter approached their table.

Myrtle said, "I'll have a Blonde Dubonnet, please."

"Gin and tonic," said Miles to the waiter.

The waiter nodded and hurried away.

Myrtle attempted a softball approach to conversation with Terrell. "I hear the fish were biting today?"

"Yes. Yes, indeed they were. A decent catch, wouldn't you say, Miles?" said Terrell.

"I was pleased with it," said Miles. "It will be nice to have some salmon at home to remind me of the trip."

Terrell nodded and then returned to his crossword, clearly indicating that it was a good deal more interesting than his current companions.

Myrtle was scrounging for conversational topics, but came up with nothing. She opened her eyes wide at Miles to say that he needed to come up with some sort of small talk.

Miles cleared his throat and said, with some effort, "The weather is rather nice today, isn't it? So good to see the sun. Much better than Juneau, wouldn't you say?"

Terrell grunted. Myrtle sighed.

Fortunately for them, the waiter arrived with their drinks. Even more fortunately, a middle-aged woman with attractive features and a nice smile approached their table. Her effect on Terrell was like night and day. He immediately stumbled to his feet. Miles, always the gentleman, rose too.

"Donnice!" Terrell gasped. Pearls of perspiration beaded his forehead.

The woman beamed at him. "Hi, Terrell." Donnice glanced shyly at Myrtle and Miles and held out her hand to both of them for a handshake. "So good to meet you," she said. To Terrell, she said, "Shall we meet after my excursion? For dinner?"

Terrell stammered out a positive response, gaping at her.

"Wonderful," she said, a dimple flashing as she smiled. "It's nice to have something to look forward to."

As Donnice left, Myrtle marveled at the change in Terrell's overall demeanor and mood. He sat up a bit straighter, smiled more, and seemed confident and relaxed. Myrtle and Miles raised their eyebrows at each other. Their conversation appeared to have reached a turning point.

Terrell immediately became more animated. He demonstrated his catches to Myrtle with what sounded like a minimum of hyperbole. He seized on the topic of the weather with renewed enthusiasm as he pondered on the at-sea day they had tomorrow and how the weather would be for it. And he even, finally, broached the topic of Eugenia.

"Was there any mention of a memorial service for Eugenia?" he asked. "From the ship's chaplain, I mean. He was the one who organized it the last time. For, uh, Mother. I wanted to make sure to make it to a service, but my schedule appears to be filling up faster than it had earlier in the trip." He blushed again.

The blushes made him look a good deal younger and more vulnerable. Myrtle wondered how much romantic experience he actually possessed. It certainly appeared to be very little. But if his mother had orchestrated his courtship to his ex-wife, he could have skipped the whole courtship process the first time around.

Terrell had looked at Miles when he asked the question. Miles said, "Not that I've heard, but I would only have heard through the grapevine. Maybe Bettina or someone would be a better person to ask." Miles shifted uneasily as he said Bettina's name. He never enjoyed being pursued.

Myrtle said, "I'm sure the chaplain is putting something together—it will likely be during tomorrow's at-sea day."

"Good point. It would be perfect for a day with no excursions. I'll be sure to be there. The poor girl," said Terrell. He took a small sip of his beverage.

Myrtle said, "Poor girl indeed. Miles was saying that Eugenia had a crush on you."

Terrell gave a small nod. "I'm afraid so. It was nearly impossible to escape her sometimes. I felt that, no matter where I was, I'd look up, and there would be Eugenia staring all goo-goo eyed at me."

"Really? I wouldn't have imagined that were true at all," said Myrtle. "Every time that *I* saw her, she was waiting on your mother hand and foot."

"I wish that *had* been the case. It seemed to me as if she were around every corner, peering at me," said Terrell, a trace of the old grouchiness in his voice.

Myrtle wondered if Eugenia were peering around corners trying to make sure Terrell *wasn't* there. Maybe, instead of trying to stalk him, she was really trying to avoid him. She said, "When was the last time you saw Eugenia? We were trying to piece together a timeline to help us understand when she might have died. What were you doing last night?"

Terrell took a thoughtful sip of his drink. "Let's see. Last night I attended a lecture on the ship. If you haven't attended any of the series, they have experts in a variety of different fields that give talks on their area of expertise. Highly informative. This particular talk focused on civil service reform."

Miles, out of eyeshot of Terrell, rolled his eyes at Myrtle and took a generous sip from his gin and tonic. The lecture certainly didn't sound like much of a fun time to Myrtle, either.

"After the lecture, I happened on the young woman that you just met. Charming lady. Donnice." Here, Terrell blushed again and pulled at his shirt collar. "She suggested that we have a drink together," he said in wonder. "So we did. Over by the piano bar, a very elegant spot I think and with excellent views. Lots of wildlife traipsing by the window and such."

Myrtle said, "And no Randolph there to ruin the mood? The piano bar area seems to be a favorite haunt of his."

Terrell made a face. "Fortunately, no Randolph was present. I suppose he'd stumbled off somewhere by then after an extended bar crawl. Anyway, Donnice and I had a lovely time sipping our beverages and viewing the landscapes as we cruised by. I learned that she lives only an hour away from my home! Imagine that. It certainly is a small world."

So perhaps this was more than just a shipboard romance for Terrell. He seemed to hope so and the amount of emotion he was investing in the budding relationship would indicate that.

"Donnice and I were just laughing over some witty thing she'd said when I glanced across and saw Eugenia staring at us. Staring! The poor girl appeared completely devastated," said Terrell.

Miles said, "What did she do when she caught your eye?"

"Oh, typical Eugenia stuff. Ran away like a terrified rabbit. But you know, I've been nothing but a gentleman there," said Terrell swiftly. "I never encouraged Eugenia. Why on earth would I? Although naturally, I felt bad that she was so upset. I wondered later, when the policeman was talking to me, if perhaps Eugenia hadn't decided to go for a soothing soak in the hot tub at that point. It might have settled her nerves a little and reduced some of that horrid stress I saw on her face."

"Maybe," said Myrtle smoothly. "Was it nighttime at that point? I've lost track with the lectures and drinks."

"It was probably after nine. I rather lost track of time, myself." Here Terrell flushed again.

Myrtle decided to play up to Terrell's ego again. It was fairly easy to do. "You seem to be an intelligent man who knows a lot about a variety of things. What's your understanding about Eugenia's estate and how it will be dispersed?"

"My *mother's* estate." Terrell swiftly corrected her. "Well, with Eugenia gone, it will go to probate court. I'm sure Eugenia didn't have a will and the family will argue at the court for a more just distribution of the estate to the deserving beneficiaries."

"Of whom you're one," said Myrtle.

"Of course," said Terrell with more than a hint of his old impatience. "Why shouldn't it be equitably divided among the family?"

"By the way," said Myrtle casually, "We have a witness who states that you told your mother *you'll be sorry* shortly before her death."

Terrell stared at her. "Who blabbed about that?"

"Does it matter? Clearly it's true," said Myrtle.

"I only meant that I wouldn't be speaking with her if she continued interfering in my life—that I was going to attempt disconnecting with Mother. That would have been the ultimate revenge since she was always dabbling in my affairs. I certainly didn't mean that I'd be *murdering her*."

Myrtle said, "I see. One other thing, then. You indicated after your mother's death that you thought Randolph was responsible. Is that still your theory?" She took a long sip of her Dubonet.

"I certainly think that he *could* have done it. Why not? He was vocally upset about Eugenia receiving Mother's estate. And, as I mentioned before, sometimes I think Randolph takes in a lot more than we give him credit for. But I would prefer it were someone like Bettina," said Terrell.

"Why is that?" asked Myrtle.

Terrell shrugged. "I'd like these crimes to remain outside the family for publicity's sake. As a matter of fact, you may have noticed that I've become more reconciled with your sleuthing around. It's appalling that the ship or cruise line takes such a nonchalant view toward murder. The more I think about it, the more I'd like my name to be cleared. If the press gets hold of all this—which may happen since we'll be in probate court—I'll have a cloud of suspicion around me."

Miles said, "Which obviously wouldn't be good business for a physician."

"Obviously," agreed Terrell.

"But do you have any evidence against either Randolph or Bettina? I hate being tiresome, but there's no other way to clear your name but to ask tiresome questions," said Myrtle.

Terrell said, "What constitutes evidence? Does motive?"

"Sure," said Myrtle and Miles in chorus.

"As far as Randolph goes, he's completely lazy. The man never does a day of honest work. I know he'd have loved to have supported his drunken lifestyle with my mother's estate. As I mentioned before, money would be his motive. Once the estate went to Eugenia, he would naturally have moved to murder her, too. She'd have stood in the way of his putting his hands on the money, otherwise." Terrell took a thoughtful sip of his drink and then pushed it away before continuing.

"As for Bettina, that would clearly be revenge," he said. He looked at them from the corners of his eyes, enjoying the moment when he knew something that they didn't.

"Revenge?" asked Myrtle. "On her best friend?"

"Former best friend, I'm sure," said Terrell. "Oh, she put on a good show. After all, my mother had paid for this trip. Besides, she wouldn't have wanted to alert Mother that she was furious with her. No. Because that would mean that Mother wouldn't let her guard down enough so she could kill her."

Miles said, "And this has to do with Bettina's relationship, something like that?"

"*Exactly* like that," said Terrell. "Bettina is something of a goldminer. When she finds a good prospect, she goes all out to charm him. But security is important to her and she no longer works or has any source of income other than social security and my mother."

Miles gave Myrtle a resigned look as he heard about Bettina's hunting of eligible men.

Myrtle ignored him and said, "Then why kill your mother if she were helping to support her?"

"Because my mother also decided to completely destroy Bettina's latest relationship. Bettina had made quite the conquest this time and the gentleman was a man of some means. Mother took it in her head to lure the gentleman away from Bettina." Terrell noticed the somewhat doubtful expressions on Myrtle's and Miles's faces. "I know she may not have made the most of her looks, but believe me, Mother could be a charmer. Besides, she also told horrible stories about Bettina and her motives. She made it appear that the man would look foolish to the rest of the world if he married Bettina," said Terrell.

Terrell said, "And then she even brought letters between the man and herself onboard the ship."

Myrtle added, "Do you think that your mother *wanted* Bettina to see the letters?"

"I have wouldn't put it past her," said Terrell coolly. He glanced at his watch. "And now, if you'll excuse me, I think I should get ready for my dinner with Donnice."

Chapter Twelve

Myrtle glanced at her own watch as Terrell hurried away. "How much getting ready is he going to do? Supper is hours away."

"Well, clearly he wants to put his best foot forward," said Miles. "It's really sort of sweet in a way. He's so flustered over it and is obviously no dating expert."

Myrtle nodded and finished her Dubonnet. "It does look as if he's finally coming out of his shell now that the commanding and controlling presence of his mother is gone. Which really does make me wonder if he had been desperate to get rid of her and finally start his life."

"And I suppose, if he *did* kill her, having the extra money from her estate would have helped him in his quest to start over," said Miles. "Although, as a doctor, he was certainly rich enough."

Myrtle shrugged. "It's the difference between being very comfortable and being wealthy."

"I don't know. I think rich is rich."

Myrtle said, "It's the difference between a mountain house with a river view and a house on the beach."

"I guess you're right."

Myrtle said, "On a different topic, since we've now established that supper is hours away, what are your plans for the interval?"

"I was going to try out the yoga class. It's supposed to be wonderful for joint pain and I've had a little of that in the last day," said Miles.

Myrtle said with a smirk, "You should relax in the hot tub for a while then."

"No thanks," said Miles. "Do you want to try out the class with me?"

"I'll pass. I didn't bring exercise clothes, and besides, yoga is not really my thing. Doing dog-in-the-manger and deer-in-the-headlights and all those sorts of poses," said Myrtle.

Miles said coldly, "I'm guessing you're referring to upward facing dog and the deer pose."

A voice behind them said cheerfully, "Yoga? Are you going too, Miles?"

It was Elaine. She was in high spirits, which likely meant the dawn of a new hobby for her. Red was holding Jack's hand and was right behind her.

Miles said, "I'm going, but Myrtle is pooh-poohing it."

"I'm not *really* pooh-poohing it. I've nothing against yoga, but I'm certainly not wearing regular clothes to the class. You're going, Elaine? And how was your pottery class?" asked Myrtle.

Elaine beamed at her, "I'm going to yoga. And the pottery class was fantastic! It's really inspired me, too. Oh, I've dabbled in pottery before, but I don't think I had very good instruction. Now I feel equipped to go back to Bradley and start making pots again!"

Red, behind her, rolled his eyes and gave his mother a long-suffering look. Elaine hadn't hit on the perfect hobby yet but appeared determined to keep searching for it. In some ways, it was inspiring. In others, it was a bit dispiriting.

"Tomorrow, I'm heading back to the class to paint the pots I made," said Elaine. "It's our at-sea day, so it's perfect—no excursions to go on."

Red said, "Do you know when that is, Elaine? I wanted to attend the memorial service that the chaplain is putting together tomorrow morning for Eugenia."

"The pottery painting is late-afternoon, so that's perfect," said Elaine.

It occurred to Myrtle that the dinner that night was the ship's formal night. "Do you need me to watch Jack tonight for you so you can dress up and go to one of the nicer restaurants?"

Red made a face. "Thanks, but no thanks. I'd rather skip dressing up and go to the buffet."

"Thanks, though," said Elaine. "Although now I think I'd better head out and get ready for yoga."

"Me, too," said Miles, standing up. "And I'm sure to end yoga feeling extremely relaxed for dinner."

"Especially since you've already had a drink before yoga," observed Myrtle.

Miles was wearing a dark suit when he knocked on her door later for supper. He did not even look particularly dressy to Myrtle since he always looked dressed up. On the other hand, she felt very dressed up in black slacks and a silver top. Myrtle almost felt as if she should be receiving tea with the queen.

When they were seated in the main restaurant, Miles and Myrtle looked around them. People had taken the directive to wear formal clothes in very different ways. Some were wearing blue jeans and nice tops. Some were wearing evening gowns.

And then there was Maisy. Myrtle poked Miles and gestured across the room. "Look who's coming in."

"And look what she's wearing," said Miles.

"I suppose when the cat's away, the mice will play," said Myrtle. "Her mother certainly wouldn't have wanted Maisy to wear a low-cut, strapless cocktail dress with a tiered skirt that's only thigh-length. She looks like a refugee from the 1980s."

Miles said, "I think in some ways it's rather brave that she would have packed like she did when her mother was alive and well. She didn't know her mother was going to die, after all."

"Didn't she? I haven't completely eliminated her as a suspect yet, Miles. I haven't eliminated *any* of them, actually." Myrtle observed Maisy more closely. "The dress isn't awful; it's just awful on Maisy. There comes a point where dressing younger than you are makes you look a good deal older. I think Maisy has reached that point."

"She appears to be looking for a place to sit," said Miles. He stood up, caught Maisy's eye, and motioned her to join them.

"How gallant of you, Miles," murmured Myrtle.

Miles said, "She reminded me of high school days when kids would be desperately looking for someone to sit with in a sea of unfriendly faces."

"And how clever of you to find a way to subject her to our relentless questioning," said Myrtle.

"Honestly, I think she's simply relieved to have someone to eat with. Otherwise she'd be heading back to her room to change and eat at the buffet."

Maisy indeed appeared relieved when Miles pulled out a chair for her. "Thanks so much. My date is feeling under the weather and I'm on my own. Who knows where the rest of my party is?" Her tone suggested that she didn't really care.

Relieved or not, there was also something a wee bit guarded about Maisy that night. Myrtle decided to wait until a couple of drinks had been drunk and they'd all had a chance to enjoy the four-course meal.

Maisy was looking far more relaxed by the time desserts were arriving at their table. After Maisy had taken the first bite of her chocolate cheesecake, Myrtle said innocently, "Are you planning on going to Eugenia's service tomorrow?"

Maisy made a bit of a face but didn't try to avoid answering the question. "I suppose I should. Mother would have wanted me to, I know. Did we ever hear what time it was to be? Ridiculously early, I guess?"

"I don't think it's going to be *very* early. Probably something like eleven o'clock. I don't think we've heard the exact time yet," said Myrtle. She had a couple of vanilla petit fours on her plate that she wasn't completely sure how to approach. Pick it up? Use a knife? Attempt to put the entire thing in her mouth? They were almost too pretty to eat with their pink and white edible flowers on top.

Maisy gave Myrtle a reproving look. "That's very early. But I'll go, of course. I didn't really have anything *against* Eugenia." Her expression told a different story, however.

"Miles and I were trying to figure out the last time we saw Eugenia since my son was hoping to establish time of death. It's tricky in a hot tub, you know," said Myrtle. "When was the last time you saw her?"

"Oh, I don't know. I wasn't trying to keep an eye on her, you know. I've been trying to take advantage of my time on the cruise," said Maisy, delving into her cheesecake with gusto.

Miles gave Myrtle a wry look that said Maisy was succeeding.

Myrtle persisted, though. "What did you do that evening? When we were in Juneau?"

"I turned in early. Lots of late nights will catch up with me after a while," said Maisy.

Myrtle stifled a sigh. Trust Maisy to get short-winded *now* when they were asking questions. She certainly had plenty to say earlier in the meal when she was talking on and on about her privileged childhood and how she'd had a pony named Prince.

"So you have no idea who might have killed Eugenia?" asked Myrtle. "Because it was a very violent death, you know. Was there anyone who you think could be capable of that? And why would they have done it? She seemed like a sweet, harmless little thing."

Here Maisy's eyes flashed with a show of temper. "She might have seemed that way, yes. She seemed that way to Mother. Mother thought that Eugenia was a much better-behaved person than I was. I thought Eugenia just had much less personality than I did. She was more bland."

Myrtle tried to tease more of an answer out of her. "More bland. That makes a lot of sense. I'll admit that I didn't get much of a sense of a personality from Eugenia. But who would have wanted to murder her? Such an insipid person wouldn't have inspired violence from many people."

Maisy took the last bit of her cheesecake and pushed the plate away from her. She said, "I still think Randolph might have done it. He always thought that he was going to be Mother's heir. He could have murdered Mother and then murdered Eugenia—she probably saw something and he had to get her out of the way. Besides, I saw him out really late that night that Eugenia died. I'm like Terrell—I'm not sure that Randolph is always as intoxicated as he makes out."

Myrtle said smoothly, "You saw Randolph out really late? But you just said that you turned in early that night."

Maisy had the grace to blush. "I did. But ... well . . . I left my purse at dinner by accident. I didn't realize until I was back in my room and in the bed. You know how sometimes your mind replays the day and you remember things?"

Maisy seemed to be groping for an explanation. It didn't sound all that plausible to Myrtle. If she'd remembered the purse right after she turned in and she turned in 'very early,' then how did she see Randolph out 'very late?'

They were momentarily interrupted by a silky voice. "Hi there, Miles," purred Bettina, wearing an off-the-shoulder black gown. "I was looking for you. Can we meet up for a drink after dinner? I wanted to find out all about your life as an architect. I'm always so interested in hearing about professions like yours. I was an interior designer and I think the two jobs go hand in hand, don't you?"

Miles shot Myrtle a furious look at the mention of the word *architect*. "As a matter of fact, I was an engineer, not an architect."

"Even better," said Bettina smoothly. "I do love hearing about things being built."

A red flush was creeping slowly up Miles's neck as Maisy and Myrtle looked on in interest. "I was thinking about ... erm ... having an early night."

Here Myrtle kicked Miles sharply under the table, making him grunt. She wanted to horn in on their drink, although she wasn't going to let Bettina know that. Miles had fortunately been her friend long enough to be able to correctly interpret her kick. "But," he amended reluctantly, "I'm happy to have a drink with you before I do."

"Excellent!" said Bettina with a toothy grin. "Let's meet in the piano bar at eight then?" And she sailed off with Miles looking at her unhappily as she went.

Myrtle tried to pick back up on their thread of conversation. "Let's see. What were we saying? Oh, that's right, I remember. What was Randolph doing when you spotted him?" "Looking sneaky. Furtive. Like he was up to something," said Maisy, decidedly.

Miles said, "Could he have been doing anything else? Surely he wouldn't be obviously furtive if he were planning to kill Eugenia?"

Maisy gave him an impatient look. "How should I know? I guess he could have been heading to the ship casino. He's a gambler, did you know that?"

This came as news to Myrtle and Miles. Myrtle said, "No. Every time we saw him, he was half-asleep in a chair with a drink."

"Well, anytime he's *not* passed out, he's probably in the casino. Habitual gambler. In fact, he was really racking up debts before we went on vacation. Mother was always yelling at him. In many ways, it was a relief, since it meant that she wasn't yelling at *me*," said Maisy.

Myrtle said slowly, "So if he had a lot of gambling debts, it could have meant that he owed money to people who would put a good deal of pressure on him to pay them back."

"Sure. There's your motive right there. Money. He never took Mother seriously when she threatened to write him or any of us out of her will and that was a huge mistake on his part. He should never have underestimated her. He probably got desperate for cash and decided to hurry things along. Then he would have needed to get rid of poor Eugenia since she stood between him and his money." Maisy finished off her drink. She gave a searching gaze across the restaurant as if looking for better prospects to sit with.

Myrtle had finally used a knife and fork to cut into the petit fours. She swallowed it down and said, "Have you noticed Eugenia having some sort of a crush on Terrell?"

Maisy snorted. "Absolutely not. That little mouse? More likely she was trying to avoid my brother. Who told you that— Terrell? He's got a huge imagination for someone who can be so dull. I had to give him a hard time yesterday, but seriously. He was going to sit in a library and do crosswords when he finally had the chance to get out from under his mother's thumb? I thought he was being foolish. And maybe he listened to me for once because I saw him with a girl later on."

"He does seem to be having a shipboard romance," said Myrtle. "And you're sure about Eugenia?"

"Eugenia wouldn't have dared to try to have a relationship with Terrell. That was one reason why she was never getting anywhere in life—she never took risks. Never tried to be better than she was. Now me, on the other hand, I'm trying to take advantage of this tragedy and make the best of it. Maybe that sounds awful, but surely it's the healthiest thing to do. I was stifled for years by Mother and now I have a chance to spread my wings a little. I'm taking it," said Maisy. She stood up and looked at Miles. "You should do the same—with Bettina. See you both later."

Chapter Thirteen

Miles was glum as he took the last bite of his chocolate gateau. "Do I really have to have a drink with Bettina, Myrtle? She may get the wrong impression."

"She will *not* get the wrong impression. I won't allow it. I'm going to have a drink *with* you and ask questions. There will be nothing in the least that could be considered romantic about any of it."

Miles glanced at Myrtle's plate. "Didn't you like your dessert?"

"It baffled me. I don't like it when my food is confusing. It didn't seem to want to be eaten," said Myrtle. "I cut one with my knife and fork, but the reward didn't seem worth the labor. That will teach me to order anything with a French name. I need to eat desserts with names like *cheesecake* or *pudding*."

Miles pushed his plate away and then stood, courteously holding Myrtle's chair as she rose. "Speaking of pudding, I wonder how things are going at home. With Dusty and Puddin."

Myrtle made a face. "How do you *think* they're going? When the cat's away, the mice will play. I've a feeling that Puddin is sitting in my den, fending off Pasha, eating the remains of my food, and watching *Tomorrow's Promise*."

"Dusty is more industrious, though," said Miles.

"Is he? Give him half a chance to be lazy and he'll jump on it like fleas on a hound dog," said Myrtle. "They're probably letting everything in the house and yard go until right before we get back. Then they'll scramble like crazy to have it look good. We'll have to bring our neighbors little gifts to make it up to them when we return."

Miles, who liked everything done in a particular way, looked uncomfortable at the thought of his yard resembling a South East Asian jungle. Or perhaps he was still wrestling with the fact that he was about to have a drink with a woman for the first time in a while.

Myrtle had to give Bettina credit. She'd thought of everything. She was sitting at a small table in the piano bar where the lighting was excellent. Her dress played up her figure and she was expertly made up. The pianist was playing *As Time Goes By* from *Casablanca*. And there were only two chairs at the little table. At least, there were only two chairs until Miles quickly pulled another out for Myrtle.

Bettina smiled toothily at Miles and then gave Myrtle a clear *back-off* look, which Myrtle blithely ignored. "Hi there, Bettina," she said beaming. "What a treat to hang out with you a little while. Don't we all look amazing? We should dress for supper every night."

Bettina continued shooting daggers with her eyes at Myrtle. "Yes. Miles, you look very handsome, as usual," she crooned.

Miles looked miserable and stayed as close to Myrtle as he possibly could. A waiter hovered for drink orders and Myrtle ordered a Shirley Temple. Miles waved the waiter away.

"Unfortunately," said Bettina, "this is a table for two." She was as pointed as she could be.

"Very true. We should move to a larger table," said Myrtle.

Miles, who just wanted to get the whole thing over with, said quickly, "This is fine for the short time we'll be here. As I mentioned, I do want something of an early night."

This statement appeared to make Bettina deeply unhappy as the waiter brought Myrtle her drink.

Miles gave Myrtle a small kick under the table to prompt her to get on with it. Myrtle supposed that the pleasantries could be dispensed with since she'd already spent the morning with

Bettina on the trolley. She raised her glass with its non-alcoholic beverage. "A toast! To new beginnings!"

Miles gave her an incredulous look and rested his head in his hand. Bettina raised her glass and smiled at Myrtle for the first time.

Myrtle said, "Because new beginnings are important, aren't they? I couldn't help but notice how happy Terrell was today. He's got a new lady friend named Donnice."

Bettina snorted. "Which is completely amazing. He's not exactly the sort to make new relationships happen."

"Well, this one seems to be off to a good start, although he does have old habits that get in his way, I suppose. He was apparently attending some sort of very dry lecture last night instead of partying on board," said Myrtle.

Bettina raised her eyebrows. "Maybe he did attend the lecture, but it certainly wasn't for very long. I saw him quietly escaping from the room where it was being held. In fact, he made some sort of comment about the content of the lecture being interesting, but the delivery being dull. I was on my way out to the disco room and told him he should give dancing a go. Not that he listened to me. Maybe that's when he met up with his new friend." She grinned at Miles. "*You* should try the disco room, too. You'd be surprised how much fun it is."

Miles cleared his throat. "You're right. I *would* be surprised." He gave Myrtle another desperate, light kick under the table.

"So Terrell wasn't really occupied for very long at the lecture," mused Myrtle.

Bettina said, "Exactly. So who knows? He could have found the time to follow Eugenia and knock her off. I guess the poor child could have seen something incriminating, I don't know."

Myrtle said, "You don't seem to have a problem pointing the finger at Terrell."

"Not at all. He has never been the warmest member of the family, although now I guess he's got a second chance at life. I did enjoy Celeste and found her a lot of fun to be with, but she could be very hard on her family. She was definitely hard on Terrell. Celeste always had preconceived notions about what his life should be like. She wanted him to be a doctor, a well-respected member of the community, with a nice house and yard and a nice wife. I don't think Celeste ever asked what *he* wanted," said Bettina.

Miles said, "To be fair to Celeste though, wasn't it Terrell's job to protest? Isn't that what adolescence is all about? Rebellion?"

"Terrell never really *had* an adolescence; not in the true sense of the word. He was too busy in science camps and in camps for the gifted and all the special opportunities that Celeste put together for him. Maybe he's making up for lost time now," said Bettina. Myrtle noticed that Bettina nearly imperceptibly moved her chair closer to Miles as he glanced out the window when several other passengers excitedly reported a whale.

Myrtle said, "I've been hearing that Eugenia had a crush on Terrell. Had you seen any evidence of that?"

Bettina considered this. "I don't know. I wouldn't have said so. Eugenia acted nervous around *all* the members of the family. Maybe someone misunderstood what emotion she was demonstrating and thought she was interested in Terrell. But as far as I could tell, Eugenia was just shy around him and tried to avoid him as much as she avoided the rest of the family. Besides, she's a close relative."

Myrtle asked, "When was the last time you saw anyone the night Eugenia was killed?"

Bettina said promptly, "It was probably eleven o'clock and I saw Terrell out." She held out her hands. "It seems obvious enough, doesn't it? Eugenia knew something and whatever she knew it made Terrell anxious enough to murder her." She slid even closer to Miles.

Miles quickly said, "Unfortunately, I'm fighting off a terrible headache." He gave Myrtle a hard look.

Myrtle said, "One of your migraines is it? Then you should definitely turn in. Sorry, Bettina, it looks as if we're no fun at all."

Bettina made a face. "You're certainly not. What's more, all you can talk about is murder. Miles, I look forward to finding out more about your engineering background and education tomorrow. Maybe we can even discuss books."

As Myrtle and Miles walked away from the piano lounge, Miles murmured, "Book club with Bettina. How thrilling. The book she chooses will likely be *How to Marry a Millionaire*."

"At least she reads. Or *says* she does," said Myrtle. "Although I do think it's peculiar how everyone wants to discuss books with us. What did you think about everything we've heard so far? Got any gut reactions?"

"My gut reaction is that I should take off at a trot every time I spot Bettina," muttered Miles.

"*Besides* that. It sounded as if everyone was running around the ship late last night and had every opportunity to kill poor Eugenia," said Myrtle.

"Isn't it funny how everyone says *poor Eugenia*?" mused Miles. "She wasn't actually poor at all, was she?"

"Not by the end of her saga, no. Except for the fact that everyone was contemplating murdering her. So, let's see. After polling Maisy and Bettina, they were both pointing fingers at Randolph and Terrell," said Myrtle.

Miles said, "I think Maisy is protecting her brother. At first she might have been pointing the finger at him, but now it sounds as if she's reconsidered and is forming an alliance. She's probably trying to remain on his good side since he seems to be the brains of the family. He can help them wade through the probate process with the will, and may even lend her money from time to time. I didn't get the impression that Maisy is actually employed."

Myrtle said thoughtfully, "You're right. I've never heard any mention of a job for Maisy. Hm. And she's not married or a mother, so what did she do with her time? Hang out with her mother? No wonder she had hard feelings toward her—I'd think spending tons of time with *anyone* could make you sick of them. Okay, so Maisy was trying to direct us to Randolph. Then we had Bettina trying to explain why Terrell was such an excellent candidate for the murderer."

"Why do you think Terrell lied to us about the lecture?" asked Miles. "Did he intend his presence there to work as his alibi? We could easily have checked and asked the instructor if Terrell left early, though."

"Yes, but you have to think like these suspects. We're not the police. Well, Red is the police, but he really doesn't have any jurisdiction here. How likely are you and I to check out alibis? And really, Terrell is the only one who's even tried to provide one ... everyone else is wandering around the ship or turning in early or whatever. But back to your original question. Why did Terrell say he was at the lecture? I'm thinking that it's just another opportunity for him to brag about something. Think about how he bragged about Eugenia's horrified face when she saw him with Donnice after the lecture. Eugenia was very likely dead then and he didn't see her at all. He's very fond of making himself look smarter or more interesting than he is. It's probably how he survived med school," said Myrtle.

"I wonder if he'd make it through med school *these* days," said Miles. "It's a lot more competitive to get in, I hear. And he *was* at the lecture. It simply must have been a lot more tedious than he thought."

"Which is totally ridiculous since the topic was on civil service. How anyone could have possibly thought *that* subject was going to be riveting, I'm not sure. So, he slipped out, and the next thing we know he was seen by Bettina. Then he was with his friend Donnice," recited Myrtle.

Miles said, "Yes. But since Red doesn't have a very accurate time of death for Eugenia, the killer could still be Terrell. He could have left Donnice, spotted Eugenia by herself, and quickly taken the opportunity to get rid of her."

"Or maybe he could have left the lecture, been seen by Bettina, murdered Eugenia, and *then* have seen Donnice and joined her. I guess Eugenia either was falling asleep in that whirlpool or hot tub or whatever it's called, or the killer was very quiet," said Myrtle with a frown. "I'm not totally understanding how she didn't hear someone approaching her."

"The water is fairly loud in those hot tubs with the jets going," explained Miles. "It makes a sort of white noise. I don't think anyone would hear someone else approaching. If the murderer came up behind her, they could easily have surprised her."

Myrtle raised her eyebrows. "It sounds as if you've been visiting the hot tubs. I'm sure our friend Bettina would love to join you on your next expedition."

Miles colored. "And I'd be most grateful if you'd help me avoid that woman. There's nothing like being pursued. I don't think my modest lifestyle and quiet existence is what Bettina is looking for."

"Probably not. I'll have to play up how boring you are and perhaps she'll lose interest. Pity she's a fan of our soap opera or I'd play up that angle and nearly *anyone* would lose interest in you. Speaking of Bettina, though, what do you think of the whole revenge thing? For Celeste's murder, I mean," said Myrtle.

"It sounds like a plausible motive for murder to me," said Miles. "Particularly since we've seen for ourselves how single-minded Bettina can be when it comes to a romantic interest." His flush deepened a bit. "I'm thinking that she'd found a good prospect and Celeste was jealous and decided to break things up."

Myrtle nodded. "That must have infuriated her. Everything was going along fine and dandy and Bettina was seeing a secure future and the next thing she knew, Celeste messed everything up. Or, rather, the man broke things off and Bettina was at first baffled ... until she found out while on this cruise that Celeste was behind it all. Of course, she would have wanted to strike back at Celeste."

"Exactly. But how did she strike back at her? Did she just pull a silly prank with ink? Or did she also *plan* on killing her friend ... and then she *had* to kill Eugenia because of what she saw?" asked Miles.

"I'm not sure. And I'm not really sure about Maisy, either. I do have some sympathy for Maisy—she had no life whatsoever. Her mother controlled everything, even down to her clothing. She wasn't even allowed to be an adult at all. Unfortunately for Maisy, she decided to finally rebel and spread her wings while on a cruise—a cruise where her mother ends up murdered. And we were all party to seeing her rebellion. It makes her a very obvious suspect," said Myrtle.

Miles said, "I'm not sure that Maisy would have been able to carefully execute a murder in advance. But Celeste's murder could have easily been something that took place spontaneously, after all."

"An impulsive murder would be a better fit for Maisy, for sure. Maybe Celeste summoned her to her cabin for some petty reason or other. Probably to yell at Maisy for some shortcoming or other. They could have argued. That champagne bottle was *right there* and it was incredibly heavy ... heavy enough to kill someone," said Myrtle.

Miles said, "The amazing part of the whole scenario is that Maisy wouldn't have freaked completely out after killing her mother. I can easily see her screaming bloody murder and running out of her mother's room with mascara streaming down her cheeks."

"Hmm. I can picture that, too. But maybe she's slightly more even-tempered than we realize. Or perhaps she didn't just lift the bottle with absolutely no malice aforethought. Maybe she knew *exactly* what she was doing when she picked it up. Then she might have felt *very* calm. And, if we think about it, our murderer would need to be someone who could remain calm. Eugenia's death was opportunistic from the aspect that no one knew she was going to be in the hot tub, but it still required the killer to think through the crime," said Myrtle.

Miles said, "And then we have Randolph." He shook his head. "Honestly, Randolph seems so completely incompetent to me that I have a hard time visualizing him being able to pull off two murders without being caught."

"You've always had something of a mental block against suspecting him. But think about it—he had plenty of motive to commit these crimes. We're hearing now that he's a gambler. Celeste and Randolph *met* each other in Las Vegas. Regardless, it doesn't seem as if he's very responsible when it comes to money. We've both seen him drink his money away. What if he *is* a serious gambler and he's in major debt? Murder sure would seem attractive as a quick way of solving that problem. As far as the drinking goes, we keep hearing that maybe he's faking some of the intoxication that we're seeing and is using it as a smokescreen. He could be completely lucid and just trying to use his drinking as a sort of weird alibi ... that he isn't capable of murder because he's so incapacitated by alcohol."

Miles said wryly, "Well, he certainly drinks enough to be practically immune to the stuff. I'd be falling under the table if I drank a quarter of what he does. So it sounds as if we need to follow up with him on the gambling and so forth."

"Exactly. He needs to be the next person we speak with. I wonder if he even participated in the formal night?" asked Myrtle.

"If he did, he's probably not going to spend it in the restaurant. He's most likely at one of the bars," said Miles. "As usual."

Myrtle squinted as they walked slowly up to an area with a couple of chairs and a small sofa. "Isn't that Randolph? That dissolute figure slumped in his chair?"

"It sure is. If he's not intoxicated, then he must sleep an awful lot," said Miles.

"But he doesn't really sleep, remember? He's an insomniac like we are. The only difference is that he takes lots of naps during the day."

"And night," observed Miles. "Should we talk to him now? Will he even make a lot of sense if we talk to him now?"

"I think he *always* makes sense. And we'll at least have the opportunity to catch him off-guard, which will be more challenging when he's sober. Let's try it," said Myrtle.

Chapter Fourteen

Randolph did indeed seem at least partially lucid. He raised his glass in a mock toast as Myrtle and Miles approached. "My old friends," he said, half-standing in a courteous manner. At least he attempted the half-standing crouch, until he wobbled so much that he dropped back into the armchair again. "Good to see you. But then, I do usually run into you at night, don't I. You don't sleep either, is that it?"

Myrtle shrugged as she and Miles took the other seats in the little conversation area. "We sleep sometimes, just not others. I've found that the best thing for me to do when I can't sleep is to get up and be productive."

Randolph raised his eyebrows archly. "Really? I've found quite the opposite. I take the opportunity to rise and have another drink in the hopes of relaxing myself."

"Oh no," said Miles, sounding rather scandalized. "The doctors say that's definitely *not* what we should do. Alcohol disturbs our sleep patterns."

Myrtle decided to wrest the conversation from Miles, who was beginning to sound more of an old woman than *she* was. "Being productive might prove a good alternative for you, Randolph. I'll get up and do some rote things around the house. Sometimes, at home, I'll even walk down the street to Miles's house and we'll have a coffee."

Randolph said, "Yes, but who would I talk to? Everyone I know would be asleep. That's the problem with being an insomniac, isn't it? You keep a different schedule." He looked thoughtfully at Myrtle and Miles. "You're very lucky and I don't think you even realize it. A friend to be awake with; imagine that.

I always feel like I'm haunting a house when I'm the only one awake. It's a very ghostly feeling. Perhaps that's why I turn to alcohol. Even here, even on this ship, most people turn in at some point, even the crew."

Myrtle decided to try to segue into asking questions. "You can do other things, you know. You can think. I spend a good deal of time thinking."

Randolph's mouth twisted into a smile. "Maybe you spend too much time in your own head. We can. I don't particularly like myself so I'd rather not spend too much time with my thoughts. Although it seems like I still do, no matter what. And will even do more now that Celeste is gone." He looked curiously at Myrtle. "What sorts of things do you think about? You're not trying to solve the world's problems, are you? Attain world peace; cure cancer? So ... what?"

"No, no, they're all very small problems and very local to me. How to avoid my nosy and atrocious neighbor, Erma. How to keep crabgrass from creeping into my yard and squirrels out of my birdseed. Who I'll badger to drive me to the grocery store. How to keep my tomatoes watered even when I'm out of town. On the ship, though, they've been larger problems. Who has been killing members of your family?" said Myrtle.

Randolph's eyes grew sharp and Myrtle agreed with all the family who thought he wasn't as intoxicated as he always appeared. He said, "Indeed. It's quite the puzzler, isn't it? And I've got a notion that you and your friend are very adept at solving puzzles."

Myrtle attempted and failed to look modest. Miles continued blinking owlishly at Randolph.

Randolph took a sip from the dregs of his glass and Myrtle realized that he wasn't quite ready to comment on the elimination of his family on the ship. She chose a different tack. "You said you didn't like yourself much. Why is that?"

Randolph sighed. "Oh, where to start? There's the fact that I married for money, instead of love, for one. Society rather frowns on that. Probably provided me with a lot of bad karma."

Miles appeared somewhat shocked. Myrtle frequently wondered how Miles had gotten as old as he was and remained as naïve as he sometimes appeared. Miles said, "You must have cared for Celeste, though, surely."

A faint smile played around Randolph's lips as he studied Miles. "I didn't want her *murdered*, if that's what you're asking. But no, I didn't really *care* for Celeste, as you put it. Or, if I did, I was roughly disabused of that notion after weeks of being yelled at and put down. It sort of stomps the affection out of one. Trains you *not* to like the person. Did I respect her? Yes. And I admired her intelligence and wit. But her most appealing attribute was her money. There, I've admitted it. Relief."

Randolph didn't seem relieved, though; he seemed uneasy with his admission. He seemed ... guilty. Whether this guilt was a result of feeling bad for having married for money or for something else, it was impossible to say.

Myrtle prompted, "You said you weren't sure where to start. Is there *more* that you don't like about yourself?"

Again Randolph smiled, although it didn't reach his eyes. "Quite persistent, aren't you? I feel as if I'm in a therapy session. The next thing I know, you'll be asking me for my debit card and to check my calendar to book the next appointment." Myrtle didn't reply to this and Randolph grew quiet as he considered his own failings. "There's the gambling. I do so enjoy it, but I do so hate succumbing to its pleasures."

Myrtle said, "To me, gambling equals debt. And debt definitely isn't pleasurable to me. What's the draw? Really. It baffles me."

"Everything is the draw. The sound of coins going into slots, the lights and music from the machines. Especially the hopeful feeling—that's probably the biggest draw. That on-top-of-the-world feeling you get thinking that *this time* you're going to hit it big. Once you've convinced yourself that you're going to hit it big, you open up all the possibilities. *Everything* seems possible. You allow yourself to dream about extravagant trips or vacation homes or cars or whatever else you might want," said Randolph.

"I suppose," said Miles, sounding a bit stuffy, "that that sort of dreaming stops as the night goes on, though. Wouldn't it? As you start losing, you couldn't possibly still have the riches in mind, could you?"

"Well, you *could*. But first, you feel this desire to keep playing to make up for what you've lost. I start thinking that my luck is sure to change with that *next* roll of the dice or the next dealing of the cards. In the back of my head, I'm still thinking that once I get back to the place I started, I still have the chance to make it big. Except, apparently, my luck is second to none. My *bad* luck, I mean," said Randolph languidly.

Myrtle said, "Am I right, then? Does gambling equal debt?"

Randolph sighed. "It appears to. For me, anyway."

"Are you in debt now?" asked Miles. His tone was rather horrified. Myrtle was quite certain that Miles had never carried a credit card balance. He likely made extra principle payments every month toward his car payment or mortgage.

"Sadly, yes. I'm in debt now. Although, who knows? Maybe I'll win big tonight at the casino and pay off all my debt. You see—that's how the addiction works. It twists your mind a little. But I have to say that I think the likelihood of my winning in the ship casino is higher than the likelihood of my getting any sort of legacy from Celeste's estate." He made a face, whether at his mention of Celeste or at the will or both.

Myrtle said, "What was Celeste's attitude toward your gambling?" Although, she had a pretty good idea what it must have been. Celeste didn't suffer fools lightly.

Now Randolph made a more pronounced face. "She didn't consider it appropriate, to put it mildly. Celeste felt that gambling was beneath her; and me by extension. She thought it very common. She kept forbidding me to gamble, which only seemed to make me want to gamble more, just to defy her."

Myrtle wondered if it were even possible that Randolph could have killed Celeste so that he was free to gamble. Could he be that addicted to it? Or what if they'd been having an argument about his gambling on the ship and he struck her with the champagne bottle in a fit of anger?

"What did you do when she told you not to do it?" asked Myrtle. "Did you argue with her?"

"What's the point of that? Celeste always won. She made sure of it. Besides, she held the purse strings to a certain extent, although I had an allowance. That always drove me a little crazy: an *allowance*. As if I was some sort of gawky teenager. Did I take the allowance? Grin and bear it? I did. But I hated the way it made me feel. The allowance, by the way, wasn't large enough to support my gambling, in case you were wondering. I never complained, but I always wished there was some way to express my displeasure in a non-verbal way."

Miles said, "Myrtle is an expert at doing that. She has a large collection of yard gnomes and she pulls them out and scatters them all over her front yard whenever she's angry with her son. He lives across the street from her."

Myrtle smiled smugly. "It works, too."

Randolph smiled in return. "What a wonderful idea! Gnomes. Say, are you the person who has gnomes on your cabin door?" Myrtle nodded. "I thought they was so whimsical. And now that I know the story behind it, they're even more delightful."

Myrtle said, "It's a real testament to Red's current level of distraction that they're still on my door."

Miles was still clearly worrying about the gambling. He said, "Is the gambling debt serious? That's to say, in movies it's always a matter of life or death—you *have* to pay the bad guys back or else they'll do something horrible to you."

"Cement shoes," agreed Myrtle. "Isn't that what they always say in the movies? That they'd throw you in the lake with cement shoes on."

Randolph now looked slightly amused. "Where on earth do you think I'm gambling? I'm not involved with the mafia, you know. Most of my debts were accumulated online and then more on this ship. It's more of a *debt* problem than it is an I'm-worried-about-saving-my-life problem."

"Oh," said Miles, looking relieved. "Well, that's a good thing, anyway."

Randolph said, "And let's see. Where were we? That's right; we were enumerating all the things I don't like about myself. I think we've come to the last thing. That's alcohol."

"You do seem to like *that*," observed Miles.

"Right you are. I just don't like *myself* when I'm on it. Which is most of the time. I drink, perhaps, just a wee bit too much. But since I like so little of myself, maybe it makes sense that I spend so much of my time drinking. It makes me forget," said Randolph.

"What are your plans when you return home?" asked Myrtle.

Randolph sighed again. It was a long, gusty sigh. "It sounds as though I'll be camped out at the old homestead waiting for the probate courts to figure out what to do with this mess. Perhaps surreptitiously selling off bits and pieces of Celeste's estate for cash ... just the small bits that no one would miss or notice. One has to do something to survive in the meantime. And maybe cleaning myself up to make myself charming and presentable to some other widow of means looking for a companion. That will take some doing."

He didn't look particularly cheered by the prospect.

Miles said, "And what do you think the *rest* of the family will be doing in that interim where the courts are making decisions?"

Randolph didn't appear to be any more cheered by considering them. "Heavens. It will be something to behold, I'm sure. Maisy will go off on some sort of tear, I'm guessing. Since her mother isn't around to curb her behavior, she'll likely be doing one ill-advised thing after another."

"Would she have the income to do that?" asked Myrtle. "I'd gotten the impression that her mother was supporting her, completely."

"She was. So maybe Maisy will be there alongside me—pinching family heirlooms and selling them at pawn shops," said Randolph with a smirk. "I'll have to make sure to beat her to it. And then, let's see. Bettina wasn't counting on money from Celeste, obviously, but she'd be off hunting for a new beau since Celeste apparently ruined her last match."

Miles shifted uncomfortably in his seat.

"Then we have Terrell," said Randolph with relish. "Old Terrell, old stick in the mud. Do you know I've rallied up some sympathy for old Terrell lately? Very surprisingly."

Myrtle said, "Have you? Why?"

"I suppose because he seems vulnerable now, somehow. Now that he's out there on his own and trying to forge his own relationships. I spotted him with that new gal ... the new friend of his. Donna?" asked Randolph.

"Donnice," corrected Myrtle and Miles in chorus.

"That's right. Terrell looked like a blushing schoolboy. Quite amazing. He was always so stony-faced and solemn and completely miserable. Having his mother die was probably the absolute best thing that could have happened to that man, as terrible as it is to say. He's finally coming out of his shell. It's a pity for him that it took all the way to middle-age for him to be able to spread his wings a bit." A waiter walked by and looked expectantly at Randolph and he nodded at his glass for a refill. He gave Myrtle a smile. "Gnomes. I shall start thinking of you as the gnome lady."

"You won't be the only one," said Miles. "Myrtle has become something of a local attraction at home."

"They're perfect," said Myrtle with a shrug. "They please me and irritate my son. What could be better? But, moving on again to *your* family. Overall, what are your thoughts about the family? In light of everything that's happened on this trip, I mean."

Randolph raised his eyebrows. "Well, they're not hypocrites. I'll say that for them. They're all very relieved to have Celeste out of their hair. But, sadly, one of them is a killer. Because it's not me."

Myrtle and Miles left Randolph when his drink arrived. They'd silently and mutually decided that any additional alcohol would not help with Randolph's general coherence. Besides, they'd likely gotten everything they needed to know from him.

"So we have Terrell remaining," said Miles.

Myrtle said, "That's right. We want to follow up with him on that lecture and the fact that his alibi really isn't an alibi. I suppose he wouldn't want to speak with us if he's still out with Donnice."

"Unlikely," agreed Miles.

"In that case, I think the best time to find him is tomorrow morning. He seems to be a creature of habit, and Terrell's habit is to rise early and go to the top deck for a coffee and crossword puzzle. And we can help him out with the puzzle since he seems an inept player at best," said Myrtle with a sniff.

"I'm sure he'll be delighted," said Miles dryly.

Myrtle surprised herself by sleeping through the entire night until her alarm went off at six forty-five. It was rare for her to fall asleep and then wake the next morning with absolutely no recollection of what might have transpired for the previous seven hours. Sleeping was a gift and something she was given only occasionally. It made her quite cheerful to have gotten it. She got ready for the day with a smile on her face.

Miles was waiting for her when she walked out of her room. "Buffet first, or Terrell first?"

"Oh, I think Terrell, don't you? I'm not sure how long he'll be up there working on the puzzle. I'm imagining that he's the sort of crossword puzzler who gives up about three-quarters of the way through the puzzle." There was a slight smugness in Myrtle's voice that she couldn't quite get rid of. That was the smugness of someone who rarely found a puzzle she couldn't complete.

Chapter Fifteen

They found Terrell, as they expected, on the top deck in the ship library. Instead of puzzling over the clues, he appeared to be staring off into space. He jumped when Myrtle and Miles approached.

"Sorry," said Myrtle insincerely. "You must have been deep in thought. Trying to figure out a clue? Perhaps Miles and I can be of assistance—we're both experts with many years of experience."

Ordinarily, she'd have expected Terrell to bluster through a defensive explanation of his crossword ability, but today he seemed very absent-minded and vague. He said slowly, "Many years of experience."

"That's right," confirmed Miles. "Can we help you with something?"

Terrell immediately looked relieved. "Actually, that would be wonderful. I've been trying to figure out what to do."

"How many letters is the answer?" asked Myrtle. She started reaching for the paper.

Terrell's eyes narrowed in confusion and then he said, "Oh, you're talking about the puzzle. I was talking about some advice I need. Since, as you pointed out, you do have years of experience between the two of you."

Myrtle was tiring of the confusing conversation and was ready to go enjoy a coffee and the breakfast buffet. "What's the problem you need help with?"

Terrell blushed a bit and said, "It's Donnice. I just don't know what to do. I've never really been in a situation like this … meeting someone and making conversation and making future appointments to meet for meals and drinks and such."

Myrtle said, "You mean *dating*. That's what dating is all about. But you've been married."

"Yes, but that was Mother's idea and she arranged the whole thing. Dates, too. Now I'm on my own and horribly out of practice. I suppose I was never *in* practice and I'm certainly having to scramble now. What I want to know is, what to do to continue seeing Donnice," said Terrell.

Miles said, "You're talking about when you're back home?"

"That's right. It's amazing that she doesn't live very far from me. I mean, it's a drive in the car, but not one that would limit our seeing each other. The problem is that I don't want to seem ...." Terrell stopped and searched for the right word.

"Pushy?" asked Myrtle. Because it *was* rather pushy to try to continue a shipboard romance on the ground.

"That's right," said Terrell, relieved. "I don't want her to think that I'm taking it too seriously. In case *she* doesn't want to take it too seriously. I've been in a stew about it. What do you think I should do? Or say? I don't want to drive her off. What if I ask her for her number and she gives me a fake phone number or something, just to get rid of me?" Terrell seemed to be working himself up into a lather over it all. "And what about today? Should I ask her to go out on an excursion with me? Is that, again, pushy?"

Myrtle realized once again that Terrell had paid little attention to anything to do with the ship's itinerary. "Well, you certainly won't be asking Donnice to go on an excursion with you *today*. Not unless you both dive overboard. It's our at-sea day."

"Oh. Oh, right. Of course." Terrell looked bemused.

"But, as I recall from yesterday afternoon, *she* asked *you* to do something with *her*. So it seems only right to reciprocate today. Otherwise, your problem might be that she doesn't believe you're as serious as she is," said Myrtle.

"There are shipboard movies," suggested Miles.

"Movies," murmured Terrell as if making mental notes. "That would be easier than other activities. Maisy told me we should go dancing." He made a face. "I'm no dancer. I'm not wanting to drive her *off*. All right, so I'll be the one to suggest a mutual activity today."

"You might want to ask her questions about herself. And give her a compliment of some kind ... that her blouse really brings out the color in her eyes or some such," said Myrtle.

Terrell actually took out a slip of crumpled paper from his pocket and jotted down her suggestion on it. Miles rolled his eyes at Myrtle. This was dating 101 and Terrell acted as if the advice was something he'd never considered before. The idea that an octogenarian who hadn't been on a date in fifty years or more could advise him on dating just went to show how rusty he was.

Myrtle said, "As far as wanting to see her after the cruise, why not be upfront with her? Tell her that you don't want her to think you're taking things too seriously, but that you really enjoyed meeting her and spending time with her. That you'd like to learn more about her after you return home."

Terrell was furiously scribbling on the sheet of paper. Miles and Myrtle exchanged another glance.

Miles added, "If you thought you were being too pushy, you could give her your number and let her be the one to follow up at home. Then you'd know for sure if she were interested."

This idea seemed to make Terrell anxious. "What if she loses the number and it turns into a missed connection? Like something out of that old movie."

"*An Affair to Remember*?" offered Miles.

Myrtle said, "I hardly think that would happen, Terrell. But Miles has a point—give your number to her and then you know what her intentions are. Put *her* in the driver's seat."

Terrell suddenly turned quite pale. "Here she comes! Here she comes!"

Donnice was across the room, smiling. She lifted a hand for a friendly wave.

Miles looked alarmed. "We should go."

Myrtle shot him a look. "We have other things to discuss with Terrell."

"I don't want to be party to an intimate conversation," protested Miles, looking squeamish.

Terrell looked panicky. "You can't go! Not now. I'm all worked up. I won't even be able to say anything. Coach me through it."

Donnice paused to get a coffee from the counter on her way to join them.

Myrtle said crossly, "I'm not Cyrano de Bergerac, Terrell. And this woman is not scary, I promise you. I *know* scary. *I'm* scary. Donnice is a piece of cake."

"I'm going to give her my number now. I don't think I'll have the guts to do it later," said Terrell.

Miles shifted uncomfortably and looked longingly at the door. "I wouldn't rush things. Don't just spit it out, Terrell."

Myrtle was feeling desperate to ask her question. The barista was making a complicated drink for Donnice but it would still only likely take her a minute to get the coffee. "Terrell, Miles and I will help you. We will not desert you while you're so worked up."

Terrell said fervently, "Thanks for that. You don't know how much I appreciate it."

"Oh, I think I do. But I do have one thing that I wanted to ask you. A favor," said Myrtle.

"Of course," said Terrell in a brisk, professional voice. "What can I do for you? Some sort of medical question?"

"No. I want to know why you lied to Miles and me about the lecture. I heard that you left it early and that leaves you with unaccounted for time. I want to know what you did with that time," said Myrtle.

Miles raised his eyebrows. Myrtle was being even more direct than usual.

But Terrell was in no position to dilly-dally or beat around the bush. "I left early. You must have talked to Bettina. She spotted me after she'd been chatting up some poor sap in the pool area."

Miles gave a long-suffering sigh at Bettina's commando tactics.

Myrtle said to Terrell, "Bettina is really the one you should be asking about relationship issues. She's certainly got the practice."

Terrell rolled his eyes. "No thanks. I'll pass. But, in terms of the lecture, you're right. Fascinating lecture topic, but dry delivery. I slipped out the door when the fellow wasn't looking. No need to hurt any feelings. He'd have noticed, though—there were only two people in the audience. Imagine that!"

"Imagine," said Miles dryly.

"As I left, I thought I might try to find Donnice." Again with the blushing. Myrtle hoped that he would soon be able to stop doing that. It might be cute on a young man in the bloom of youth, but made Terrell look as if he were afflicted with some sort of unmanageable skin condition.

Myrtle said impatiently, "Yes, yes. You were looking for the girl. But you didn't immediately find her, did you? So what happened?"

Terrell sighed. "I decided to look for her in the pool area. I knew that swimming isn't so much *my* thing, but perhaps Donnice feels differently. That's when I saw her."

"You mean Eugenia," said Myrtle. "Alive or dead?"

"I presume dead," said Terrell stiffly. He glanced over at Donnice who was now paying for her coffee. "Look, I didn't say anything because I was worried I'd be misinterpreted ... as it appears I am. When I came upon her, she was very still and slumped with her head back. It looked like too uncomfortable of a position for anyone to willingly choose if they were alive."

Miles looked at Terrell with a disapproving expression. "You're a medical professional. Didn't you think to approach her and see if she were having some sort of cardiac event or something? Something that you could have tried to help her with? She was a member of your family!"

Myrtle knew that, to Miles, the worst part was that Terrell had not behaved up to the standards that chivalry demanded.

Terrell did appear to be abashed. "I know. I should have done something. If she'd been face-first in the water then I probably *would* have done something—at the very least I'd have made sure that she hadn't fallen asleep and was drowning. But there was something very ... dead ... about Eugenia when I spotted her in that hot tub. I've seen a lot of dead bodies in my time as a doctor and I guarantee you that she was already dead. There was nothing I could have done." He paused and added, as an afterthought, "But I'm very sorry it happened. I was fond of Eugenia. In my own way. Although it was rather disturbing how she kept following me around."

Myrtle sighed. "If you say so. Sometimes it's easy to misinterpret what someone's intentions are."

Miles said unhappily, "And sometimes not. Bettina has certainly made her intentions clear."

Terrell raised his eyebrows. "If Bettina has been pursuing you, you should know that she was also apparently after some other gentleman onboard. Flirting in the pool area, I believe. Heads-up."

Miles nodded miserably. "Fingers crossed she makes a match with the fellow."

"That all reminds me that I was going to take my book to the pool deck and read. Supposed to be like being on a beach. And there's a bar right there," said Myrtle thoughtfully.

Terrell said, "If you do, be sure to sit back from the edge. Bettina was rather damp and said that there were lots of kids there splashing and no parent to fuss."

"Parents these days," said Miles, shaking his head. He looked at Myrtle. "But I do have my library book to finish. Maybe we could go to the pool this afternoon?"

"Sounds good. And now I think Donnice is upon us," said Myrtle.

Donnice was in a very cheerful mood. Her eyes danced and she seemed genuinely delighted to see Terrell. "Good morning, everyone! You know, it's just so nice to see people up and about early in the morning. I've always been a morning person, but it usually means that I'm all alone when I get up." She pulled a seat from another table to join them at theirs.

Terrell seemed frozen, weighed down by the momentous question he must ask to try to maintain this emerging relationship when he got home.

Myrtle gave him an impatient look and said, "I know what you mean. Sometimes it seems as though I'm the only person in my town that's awake—except for Miles here. He's also a poor sleeper." She turned to Terrell and said peremptorily, "Terrell? You're always an early riser too, aren't you?"

He stuttered out, "Yes. I am. Mornings are good."

Myrtle sighed. For all his degrees, Terrell was apparently turning into a monosyllabic person when faced with the charming Donnice. He gave her a helpless look and she sighed once again. Myrtle supposed that she *had* made some sort of deal with him to assist him. Miles was looking longingly at the door.

"And the conversation is always fun in the mornings, isn't it? We were just having a conversation about cell phones," said Myrtle.

Terrell seized onto this conversational topic although Donnice's expression seemed to indicate that she wasn't altogether sure it was all that interesting. "Phones, right." He launched into a long, confused, and rambling monologue on phones and how odd it was for him to get used to carrying one. This led into what a technophobe he was in general. Myrtle suspected that it wasn't very good to label oneself a technophobe at Terrell's age. Miles watched disbelievingly as Terrell continued yammering.

Finally, Myrtle interrupted, as Donnice was looking increasingly bewildered at her stammering suitor. Myrtle, with much authority in her voice that she'd gleaned in her schoolteacher years, said, "All this talk of phones has reminded me that I wanted to get Terrell's number for when I got back home."

Terrell, who'd begun perspiring at his temple, gaped at Myrtle.

"Since we've become such good friends on the ship," said Myrtle pointedly. She gave Miles a suggestive kick under the table.

"Oof! Ah ... yes. I'd like Terrell's number, too. Such good conversation over, ah, crosswords. And coffee," said Miles rather lamely as he reached down to rub his shin.

Myrtle turned to Donnice and gave her one of her sweetest smiles. "Should Terrell provide you with his number, dear? Since he's distributing it to everyone?"

Donnice blushed. Fortunately for her, her blushes were much more attractive than Terrell's were. "Yes, please," she said like a child asking for a peppermint.

Terrell swallowed hard. He tried to speak, but was completely tongue-tied. He gave Myrtle a desperate look.

Myrtle added quickly, "Oh good. Terrell was just saying how he looked forward to furthering his acquaintance with you on his return home."

Terrell, still jotting down phone numbers, pulled at his shirt collar with one hand.

Donnice said, "I'm *so* glad to hear it. And glad to be exchanging numbers." She put her hand out for the piece of paper that Terrell gave her and smiled warmly at him.

Myrtle said, "Miles and I are heading out now for the buffet. Good to see both of you." And they hurried away, relieved at their escape.

"Well done," said Miles. "That was your good deed for the day."

"*That*," said Myrtle, "was my good deed for the *month*."

They had a delicious breakfast at the buffet. Myrtle really piled her plate with all the foods that she wouldn't cook for herself when she got back home. When they were done and were walking toward their rooms, Miles asked, "What now?"

"I think, sadly, that I should start organizing my things for the trip home tomorrow. Just to put the laundry in a separate bag, that sort of thing. I need to decide what to have in my carry on, too. I suppose you've already packed everything up, as compulsive as you are. So the question should really be, what will *you* be doing now?"

"Oh, you know," said Miles glumly. "Eating, gazing at the lovely scenery, and avoiding the rapacious Bettina."

"I suspect Bettina has given up completely on you. You certainly didn't provide any scintillating conversation last night. And you made it seem as though you were a hermit living in a hovel."

"You think so? Thank heaven for that," said Miles fervently. "And after your organizing, we're going to read at the pool?"

"Exactly. It shouldn't take me too long," said Myrtle.

Myrtle was thoughtfully putting her toiletries into zipper bags when there was a light knock at the door. Surely Miles wasn't back already to go read. She opened the door and peered out.

Chapter Sixteen

"Hi," said Bettina, looking chipper. "Okay that I've dropped by? I wanted to talk to you more about Miles." She raised her eyebrows as she said, "And nice door decorations, by the way."

Myrtle considered telling Bettina right there at the door that Miles was less than smitten with her. But she realized this tactic might be less than effective if she were to talk to Bettina again before the end of the cruise. She opened the door wide. "Thanks. And sure. If you don't mind my packing while we talk."

Bettina walked in and raised her carefully painted-on eyebrows. "Well. When you pack, you pack."

Myrtle glanced around the small cabin. There were items on every available surface. "Just push some of the stuff over to the side on the little sofa there. I'll sit on the bed." She sat down amid her various vitamins and continued sorting items into bags.

"Vitamins, huh?" asked Bettina, nodding her head toward the large pile on the bed. "Is that how you stay active at your age?"

Myrtle bristled a bit at the *your age*. "Eighty is the new seventy. Vitamins are good for everyone. Even my grandson takes a gummy vitamin every day."

"Oh sure, sure," said Bettina quickly.

"You wanted to talk about Miles?" asked Myrtle.

"I did. Of course, I'm still rather put out with you for destroying our tête-à-tête last night," said Bettina with a sulky expression on her face.

"For heaven's sake. Miles was tired, or not well, or whatever. He was in no mood to have a romantic interlude. I was the one who convinced him to remain out for a few minutes before he headed back to his cabin. He's hardly the life of the party,

Bettina. Are you sure that he's your type? As a matter of fact, he and I are going to join one another shortly to go read together. Read. Is this the kind of life that you want to commit yourself to? In a small Southern town?" asked Myrtle.

As she questioned Bettina, she realized that something was bothering her. There was something that she knew but hadn't yet recognized as something important.

Bettina, to Myrtle's annoyance, was picking up Myrtle's various belongings and curiously surveying them before tossing them to one side. "Bettina, I *do* have a method to my packing madness ... if you don't mind?"

"Right. Sorry," said Bettina. "I suppose you're right. It doesn't sound like Miles and I have very much in common after all. Reading isn't really the kind of activity I had in mind."

"I suppose it's not for everyone," said Myrtle graciously. Although, in her mind, she was quite critical of non-readers. And there was still something about the reading that she was trying to remember. She added absently, "I'm rather surprised that you're still interested in Miles. I understood that you had a new beau."

Bettina's eyes narrowed. "That's news to me. I've got a new *beau*?"

"Sure you do," said Myrtle. She turned away from Bettina to reach her eye drops and extra makeup that she hadn't used. "You were allegedly flirting with him on the pool deck."

And then she froze. She realized what the discrepancy was. Bettina had told Myrtle that she'd been on the way to the disco room when she'd seen Terrell coming out of the lecture early. But Terrell had said that Bettina had said she'd been at the pool and gotten splashed by some troublemaking children. That meant that Bettina had been fully dressed and wet. As one might expect to be when drowning a younger woman in a hot tub.

Myrtle gasped as Bettina leaped at her, pushing her down on the bed and grabbing a pillow. "Thought you knew," snarled

Bettina. "Nosybody. Always in everyone's business. Doesn't pay to be nosy." She pushed the pillow over Myrtle's face.

Myrtle desperately clawed on both sides of her for something to use as a weapon against the stronger woman. Her right hand closed on something narrow and long and she raised it to stab Bettina in the side.

Bettina howled in fury and released the pillow to knock the nail file out of Myrtle's hand. Myrtle shoved the now off-balance Bettina away and stumbled to her feet, backing away from Bettina to keep her in her sights.

Myrtle knew if she could just keep Bettina talking that she had more of a chance to catch her breath and regain more strength. She gasped out, "Tell me."

Bettina was amused. Her expression was very much like a cat that had a little bird it was tormenting—a cat that knew what the outcome of the hunting game would be. "Tell you what?"

"Tell me how you murdered two people," said Myrtle, trying to steady her breathing and her nerves. She played to Bettina's vanity. "You're an older woman, and one of your victims was young."

Bettina preened. "I work out. Didn't you know? Miles should have told you since I did see him in the gym a few times, although he kept to the treadmill and didn't use the weights as I did." She said in a mulling voice, "I wonder if—now that you'll be out of the way—Miles might be more interested in a relationship with me. I'll have to try it."

Myrtle worked to stay focused. "So did you simply overpower Celeste, then? I'm imagining that you caught her off-guard. Celeste underestimated you, didn't she?"

This question seemed to resonate with Bettina. "Yes. She certainly did. As I told you, I thought that my little ink prank would help me purge myself of all my feelings of rage against Celeste. I mean, what she did was truly despicable. I was on the point of becoming engaged to Jim, and he was a terrific man.

Funny, handsome, and rolling in it. I was going to be set for life. And *Celeste*! Celeste couldn't stand to see me happy. She told this guy all kinds of lies about me. The next thing I know, he wasn't even returning my phone calls."

Myrtle felt relief that her strength was surging back. Not only that, but a fair amount of adrenaline, too. "You were still filled with rage, though, weren't you? After the prank?"

"I was. Oh, it was just like Celeste to tell me while on the cruise why Jim wasn't returning my calls. She liked the fact that she'd trapped me. She was paying my ticket on the ship and I couldn't really get angry with her ... not in an upfront way. She understood the prank and accepted that as a fair reaction. I don't think for a minute that Celeste ever guessed I'd still be mad after the prank was over. But I was. I went to her cabin just to cuss her out. Just to tell her what I thought of her," said Bettina, clenching her fists in recollection.

Myrtle said, "And you did just that, didn't you. Except that Celeste wasn't chastened at all."

"Exactly. She was *smirking* at me. Celeste was very, very pleased with herself. Suddenly, I was furious. I'm usually more of a laid back person and I don't think I'd ever been this mad in my life. When people say they see red? I did it. I literally saw red. I picked up the closest thing and it just happened to be a seriously heavy champagne bottle. I swung it at her, just to see that smirk get wiped off her face," said Bettina.

"She died on impact, I'm guessing," said Myrtle. "Blunt force trauma."

"I suppose so. When I felt for a pulse, there was nothing. But then I had a problem. I had to get Celeste out of there. You hear all the time about people on cruise ships who've been drinking and end up falling overboard and disappearing. I decided that would be the best way to get rid of Celeste. I threw the bottle overboard first and then went back for Celeste."

"Who must have been pretty heavy," said Myrtle. She rested against the desk, feeling stronger every minute.

Bettina said, "She was. But you have to remember that I was still pumped with adrenaline from our argument. I dragged Celeste out to the balcony and then was able to hoist her body halfway over the guardrail. Finally, I managed, while half-standing on a deck chair, to shove her the rest of the way over."

"Of course, you didn't realize that there was a lifeboat underneath," said Myrtle. "And you couldn't hear a thump as she hit?"

"No. It was, naturally, still light outside because it's Alaska in the summer. But it wasn't broad daylight, by any means. And it was loud out there—the wind and the water. The lifeboat was pretty far down, too. I heard nothing. No one would ever have really known what happened to Celeste if her body hadn't fallen in the boat. Then I slipped out of the cabin. I didn't think anyone was the wiser," said Bettina a bit sadly.

"But someone *did* see you—Eugenia."

Bettina said, "Apparently so, although I didn't realize it at the time. And, of course, *she* didn't realize the significance of what she had seen at the time. Eugenia was always rather slow, you know. The problem was that Eugenia knew *too much*. She knew too much about everything. She knew about Celeste's and my spat because of the ink and because she helped Celeste change."

"Spat?" asked Myrtle wryly.

Bettina ignored this. "Celeste apparently told her all about it so that Celeste could have a good laugh at my expense. Too bad for Eugenia. Once she thought about the fact that Celeste had seriously wronged me and the fact that she saw me leaving Celeste's cabin at a critical time, even Eugenia was able to put two and two together."

"Pity for Eugenia that it took so long," said Myrtle. "I could tell she was onto something. I suppose she didn't want to say anything to me about it until she was sure."

"That sounds like Eugenia. Of course, by the time she *was* sure, and had told me she'd seen me, she had to go. I stalked her discretely for hours. The best opportunity was when she was in that hot tub. She was half-asleep and the noise from the jets was quite loud. And yes, she was younger, but she was caught off-guard."

"And from behind," said Myrtle, "so she would have been at a clear disadvantage for struggling."

"Precisely," said Bettina, showing her gleaming teeth in a smile.

"But you couldn't help ending up splashed, could you? Which is why you were so damp when Terrell saw you. You had to invent a quick story, didn't you? Something you thought he'd believe: that you were flirting with a man and had gotten splashed by some poorly supervised children. The only problem is that you told *me* that you'd been on your way to the disco room when you spotted Terrell," said Myrtle.

"Yes, but I needed to get some distance between myself and the pool area," said Bettina. "And who thought you'd actually be sharp enough to find a discrepancy? And now you'll have to pay for it. Killing someone who is *older* than me is definitely preferred. And ... much easier."

Bettina lunged again at Myrtle and Myrtle frantically swung her head around to look for something on the small desk to strike Bettina with. As she did, she heard—once again—exhausted psychic Wanda's dour voice: "Snow."

With perfect clarity of mind and single-mindedness of vision, Myrtle grasped the tremendous and completely inappropriate snow globe gift and walloped Bettina's head with it with all her channeled strength and panic.

And Bettina, as Myrtle had somehow known she would, went down like a rock.

As she stared, panting, at the unconscious Bettina, there was a light tap at her door.

Myrtle wildly pushed it open and looked in amazement at a sober and smiling Randolph. He was holding a small gnome in a canoe. "Hello, gnome lady. Look what I found in the ship gift shop." He moved slightly to the right to gape at the floor. "Is that ... Bettina?'

"Oh, Randolph, I'm so glad to see you. Bettina is the murderer. And I was next on her list!" said Myrtle.

Randolph put a supportive arm around Myrtle and called out in a clear, loud, demanding voice, "Red! Red Clover! Are you in your cabin?"

Red immediately appeared in the hall, an alarmed expression on his face.

Myrtle said in a tired voice, "Red, I owe you an apology. That snow globe is indeed dangerous."

Chapter Seventeen

The ship, for all its lack of law enforcement, did house a brig—really just a small, secure room. It was in this room that Bettina was placed once the ship doctor, Dr. Powers, was able to rouse her. Apparently, the fact that she was stopped in the *process* of attempting to smother Myrtle, meant that the crime would end up being reported to the FBI upon return. Although they wouldn't investigate murders, a witnessed crime-in-progress appeared to be a different matter. And, considering that the somewhat loopy Bettina had fully confessed to Red that she'd committed the other crimes (and Red had been smart enough to record her confession with his phone), the other victims would also receive justice.

Myrtle found that she was very happy to spend the rest of the at-sea day quietly in the ship library with Miles instead of discussing the murder case with Red. What's more, during the long flight back home to North Carolina, she found herself frequently falling asleep ... aside from a frenetic plane change in Dallas. Maybe it was the fact that she was modeling sleeping so well, that Jack, who was in the middle seat between Myrtle and Elaine, also slept more of the way back home. It made for a very peaceful trip back. When they got back in at night, Myrtle saw that her yard and house looked quite tidy. It made her wonder again if Dusty and Puddin had really knocked themselves out that morning and had been slack the rest of the time she was gone.

It wasn't until the day after they'd returned back home to Bradley that Myrtle resumed her regular schedule. She woke up at the crack of dawn *Eastern* Time, which was the middle of the night in Alaska. The first thing she wondered was whether Miles were also up. She decided to walk by his house to see.

Sadly, Miles's lights were out and his house was dark. Myrtle raised her hand to ring his doorbell anyway and then hesitated. Miles had said that he had *not* slept on the plane. Not one wink. Perhaps it would be better if he continued to sleep and then they could have lunch at Bo's Diner. Even better if he drove her to the grocery store afterward so that she could restock her pantry. Best of all, if after they went to the store, they watched *Tomorrow's Promise* together.

Myrtle's head was full of plans as she turned to walk back down the sidewalk toward home. Which is likely why, when a dark, furry thing brushed against her, she shrieked. Myrtle wasn't ordinarily much of a shrieker.

It was Pasha, and the black cat appeared amazingly undeterred by the loud noise her owner made as she brushed back and forth repeatedly against Myrtle's legs.

"You dear, brilliant cat!" praised Myrtle. "You knew I'd come back!"

Miles's lights were now on, unnoticed by Myrtle until his front door opened and Miles appeared, steel-gray hair standing on end, robe hastily thrown on, and glasses crooked on his nose. "Yelling," he said in a tired voice, "is an unusual wake-up tactic for you, Myrtle, but quite effective."

"As a matter of fact, I was being very thoughtful," protested Myrtle. "I was walking back home so that I wouldn't disturb you. It's only that Pasha decided to have a lovefest with me and she startled me. The darling."

Miles, who hadn't seen the black cat in the darkness, took an automatic and wary step back.

Myrtle realized an apology appeared to be in order. "Ah ... sorry about waking you up. Just go back to sleep and I'll check in with you later. I've been formulating Bo's Diner plans and soap opera plans." She carefully left out the bit about the grocery store, guessing that the errand would sound less than appealing at five a.m.

Miles said, "You should realize that's not how it works. I'm up for good now."

"Well then, follow me home. I want to feed Pasha."

Pasha led the way back, knowing that tuna was at the end of the trip. Myrtle and Miles formed a small parade behind her. As they walked up to Myrtle's house, a figure separated from the dark shadows on the porch and croaked, "Welcome home."

This time, it was Miles who shouted in surprise. Pasha hissed at him and Myrtle gave Miles a reproachful look. "Really, Miles. It's just Wanda."

Miles nodded in relief before looking alarmed again. "But it's not even dawn yet. Surely you didn't walk here all night, Wanda!"

Wanda shook her head and followed Myrtle inside before sitting gingerly on Myrtle's sofa. "Dan has a gig and has to be at the shift early. Painting."

For the life of her, Myrtle couldn't imagine Dan doing a decent painting job, but it definitely wasn't her problem.

Wanda looked solemnly at Myrtle. "You got back home."

"I did, with your help. Very prescient tip of yours, Wanda. The snow globe was the right tool," said Myrtle.

Wanda nodded. "Knew snow would be helpful. Wasn't sure how."

"Since you've had such clear sight for me, maybe you can answer a question for me. How tidy was my house and my yard while I was gone?" asked Myrtle intently.

"Mine too," said Miles quickly. "That is ... if you came by and assessed things while you were in town at the newspaper."

Myrtle rolled her eyes at Miles. He was definitely not hopping on the psychic bandwagon, despite large amounts of evidence that Wanda had a gift.

Wanda, however, didn't seem to take offense. "Didn't come by, but I know anyway. Houses and yards looked great."

Myrtle frowned. "Okay. I'm not doubting you, Wanda, but that's not exactly in line with what I'm used to from that duo."

Wanda nodded again. "Subcontract."

"What's that?" asked Myrtle sharply.

"Them subcontracted out fer it. Puddin's niece. Real good at cleaning. Real cheap, too. Even did the grass."

Myrtle and Miles stared at each other.

Myrtle said, "That Puddin and her nonsense." She took a closer look at Wanda. She looked tired, as she had before Myrtle left town. Myrtle said, "Wanda, I think you need a break. You probably could use a weekend at a spa, but that's not in either of our budgets."

Wanda nodded.

"So, as a poor but low-cost substitute, let's have you stay with me for a few days. Of course, you don't have any of your things, so we'll have to take you home to pack you a bag," said Myrtle.

Wanda lifted her bony arm and, sure enough, there was a small overnight bag hanging there.

Myrtle smiled. "Or maybe you *do* have an overnight bag. Perfect. I guess we just need to let Dan know?"

Wanda shook her head, indicating that she'd already informed her brother of her future invitation.

"Then we should move right on to a meal." Myrtle decided that she was going to ask Sloan for a raise for Wanda. Her horoscopes were popular enough to warrant it, and Myrtle had the sneaking suspicion that Wanda's income was going to overdue bills instead of groceries. As she walked to the kitchen, she wasn't exactly sure what she could create out of the contents of her kitchen. "Well, should we have some breakfast?"

Miles looked doubtful. "Have you got any unspoiled food? Or will we be forced to eat a meal created entirely out of ketchup and mayonnaise?"

"Company comin'," said Wanda gruffly.

A second later, there was a tap at the door. Miles answered it to find Red standing there. He was holding a plastic grocery bag.

"Red!" said Myrtle in surprise. "Surely you haven't converted to being an early riser?"

"No," answered Red carefully. "It's just that when people are screaming outside before dawn, we police chiefs seem to jump out of bed." He gave Myrtle and Miles a hard look. Miles blushed.

"It's all Pasha's and Wanda's fault for surprising us," said Myrtle with irritation. "You'd scream, too. But all will be forgiven if you have some sort of food source in that grocery bag."

Red grinned. "Elaine had biscuits in the freezer. I think this may be a good occasion to defrost them since you seem to be hosting a slumber party."

"No slumbering here!" protested Myrtle. "But we'll take the biscuits. Elaine is an excellent cook. Why can't she start a cooking hobby instead of trying out crafts?"

Red shrugged as he handed over the bag. "I've no idea. I could really sign onto a cooking hobby. But she's already found a pottery club of some sort, so I guess any cooking will have to wait."

"And we'll have to fill our homes with unique-looking pottery," said Myrtle with a slight shudder.

As Myrtle defrosted the biscuits in the microwave, Miles asked, "Have you heard anything about Bettina?"

Red said, "Only that she's in jail and likely to stay there. Certainly can't afford bail, and the family didn't seem particularly interested in contributing. She's confessed to the authorities anyway, so it should be pretty cut and dried. At any rate, she's in a place where she can't harm anyone else." He paused before changing subjects. "Mama, what are you doing today? Need me to run you by the grocery store?"

"Oh, no. Miles is going with me later," said Myrtle breezily.

Miles appeared surprised by, and then resigned to, this news.

"Besides, most of the day today, I'll be writing my story," said Myrtle.

Red raised his eyebrows. "Story? A helpful hints column for the paper, I hope?"

"Certainly not. Sloan practically begged me to do a travelogue of our trip," said Myrtle scornfully.

Red gave her a hard look. "Are you sure? That doesn't sound like the kind of thing that Sloan usually likes to put in the *Bugle*. He prefers the excessively local stories—little Timmy Logan's bike accident and the scar that followed. Or Horace Stringfellow's big catch out in the lake and how many pounds it was. A report on our cruise itinerary isn't remotely local."

"Wanda and I will be heading to the *Bugle* office later today," said Myrtle with a sniff as she removed some biscuits and put them on plates.

Wanda, naturally, didn't look at all surprised to hear that. It was likely why she was at Myrtle's house to begin with. She hungrily attacked a biscuit without even waiting for Myrtle to put butter out.

"Wanda will be turning in her most recent horoscopes and I will be turning in my article. My *pièce de résistance*," said Myrtle.

"Why am I not surprised by your lack of modesty?" asked Red of no one in particular.

"What's your story angle?" asked Miles.

"It will be a new type of article. A travelogue/crime story/investigative report. Cruising on the high seas with a killer ... and no cops in sight. The wild, wild west of the sea!" said Myrtle.

"I'm a cop," reminded Red dryly.

"Who frequently wasn't in my sight, so there," said Myrtle complacently.

Miles said, "It sounds like a novel. A melodramatic one."

"An unbelievable one," said Red.

But Wanda said in a knowing tone and a gap-toothed smile, "One that will be picked up on the newswire to all the papers."

Author's Note and Acknowledgments for Cruising for Murder:

Thanks so much for reading my book! I hope you enjoyed it. If you want to be notified of future releases, please subscribe to my free newsletter at: http://bit.ly/2aqzQmB

I actually took the same cruise as Myrtle and Miles in 2015. It was a fun and action-packed trip with absolutely no murders at all!

I especially loved seeing the wildlife ... and eating all the delicious food on the cruise. I took pictures of all kinds of odd spaces on the trip, knowing I'd be describing the ship a year later. Like Myrtle, I appreciated that the crew had mats with the day of the week on them in the elevator. It was easy to forget what day it was!

I have several people that I especially want to thank for helping with this book. One is John Ferrell who supplied me with some spectacular Southern names for this and future books (readers...I love great Southern names. Email me whenever you have one to share and you may see them in future books!) Thanks for your help, Johnny!

I also want to thank maritime attorney James Walker who advised me on legal ramifications of crimes at sea (or lack of legal ramifications! Were you as surprised to learn this as I was?) Any mistakes made in my text are mine alone and no fault of James.

Many thanks as always to Judy Beatty for her careful editing; Karri Klawiter for her vivid and beautiful covers; and my mother, Beth Spann, for being a great first reader with excellent suggestions. Thanks again to Amanda Arrieta for her thoughtful notes and spot-on ideas for ways to improve my stories. Thanks to Tom and Dottie Craig who not only came up with the idea of the cruise, but planned it! We had so much fun.

Thanks, also to my husband, Coleman, and children Riley and Elizabeth Ruth for their support, love, and encouragement.

The next Myrtle Clover mystery will be *Cooking is Murder*, to be released in 2017. Myrtle will try to become an even *better* cook at a local cooking class. Myrtle thinks she's already an *excellent* cook, so she enrolls to improve. Hilarity may ensue. :)

Other Works by the Author:

Myrtle Clover Series in Order:
Pretty is as Pretty Dies
Progressive Dinner Deadly
A Dyeing Shame
A Body in the Backyard
Death at a Drop-In
A Body at Book Club
Death Pays a Visit
A Body at Bunco
Murder on Opening Night
Cruising for Murder (2016)
Southern Quilting Mysteries in Order:
Quilt or Innocence
Knot What it Seams
Quilt Trip
Shear Trouble
Tying the Knot
Patch of Trouble (2016)
Memphis Barbeque Mysteries in Order (Written as Riley Adams):
Delicious and Suspicious
Finger Lickin' Dead
Hickory Smoked Homicide
Rubbed Out
And a standalone "cozy zombie" novel: Race to Refuge, written as Liz Craig

Where to Connect With Elizabeth:
Facebook: Elizabeth Spann Craig Author
Twitter: @elizabethscraig
Website: elizabethspanncraig.com
Email: mailto:elizabethspanncraig@gmail.com

Thanks!

Thanks so much for reading my book...I appreciate it. If you enjoyed the story, would you please leave a short review on the site where you purchased it? Just a few words would be great. Not only do I feel encouraged reading them, but they also help other readers discover my books. Thank you!

Made in the USA
Middletown, DE
20 August 2016